JACKIE
MANTHORNE

SUDDEN DEATH

gynergy
books

Cover illustration by: Mary Montgomery

Edited by: Jennifer Glossop

Printed and bound in Canada by: Hignell Printing Ltd.

*gynergy books acknowledges the generous support
of the Canada Council.*

Published by:
gynergy books
P.O. Box 2023
Charlottetown, PEI
Canada, C1A 7N7

Canadian Cataloguing in Publication Data

Manthorne, Jackie, 1946-

Sudden death

"A Harriet Hubbley mystery"
ISBN 0-921881-43-6

I. Title.

PS8576.A568S83 1997   C813'.54   C97-950018-4
PR9199.3.M3495S83 1997

*To Mona
and our memories of Montreal*

Contents

Harriet Hubbley dropped the packing tape and scissors and rushed past the boxes stacked almost to capacity in her living room to answer the ringing telephone.

"Hello!" she shouted into the receiver, then cursed when the message on her answering machine cut in. "Wait a minute!" she yelled, putting down the phone and running into the bedroom, where she pressed the "Stop" button on the machine and picked up the receiver. "Hello?" It was too late; the caller had hung up.

Harriet, better known to her friends as "Harry" and to the junior and senior high-school students in her physical-education classes as "The Hub," stared at the receiver for a few seconds before she replaced it. "Give me a break, will you?" she muttered as she went back to the living room and hung up the phone there. Fortunately, the phone rang again a moment later. "Hello?"

"Hey, *chérie, que fais-tu*? What are you doing? We thought you were going to have dinner with the rest of us before the reception," complained Manon Lachance.

Harry glanced at her watch and then lightly slapped her forehead. "I'm sorry, Manon, I completely lost track of the time." Manon was an old friend. They had met as students at McGill University and, like many people who have known each other for a long time, they were comfortable in their relationship. Being together didn't require much thought; they fit like feet in an old pair of slippers or a ring habitually worn on the same finger. Even when they hadn't seen each other for months, a certain intimacy was present when they met again.

"I thought I would spend a few hours packing when my session on 'High School Athletics after the Millennium' finished early this afternoon." Harry was referring to the workshop she had attended on the final day of the three-day teachers' convention which was held at Montreal's Metro Convention Centre every year in early December. "Listen, why don't I meet you at the reception at McGill around seven-thirty? That way I won't hold you up."

"*D'accord*," Manon agreed. "We'll see you at the university, then."

Harry hung up and went back into the living room. It was a mess, with empty boxes strewn all over the floor; books, magazines and knick-knacks cluttering the sofa and chairs; and bits of packing paper and tape littering the carpet. She was bushed. But she still had a lot to do before her move to Key West in January. Harry could have afforded to hire not only movers, but also packers; her first woman lover and good friend, Barbara Fenton, had died last year in Key West and had left Harry her guesthouse, Isadora's Hideaway, and investments worth around three-hundred-thousand dollars.

Harry sighed and temporarily hid the mess from view by switching off the overhead light. Her stuff wasn't going anywhere; it would certainly be waiting for her when the weekend was over.

Many teachers from out of town would leave Montreal tonight, but several of her friends from university days had decided to take advantage of the convention to hold a few of their own get-togethers, starting with the dinner she had just missed. But there were plenty of other social events on the conference program to choose from, including a day-long jaunt to the picturesque Laurentians that Saturday, with a stop for lunch at a well-known ski chalet at Mont-Tremblant, and dinner at a Greek restaurant on Montreal's ever-popular rue Prince-Arthur. From that particular restaurant, it would only be a short walk to the very French and exceedingly trendy rue St-Denis and several dozen bistros, cafés and bars, including two popular lesbian bars where those who were so inclined could dance — or cruise — the rest of the night away. Manon had agreed to host a brunch for their old friends on Sunday and, in deference to those who would close the bars at three in the morning and then go on for an early breakfast at one of Montreal's all-night restaurants, brunch was scheduled for eleven.

Harry quickly changed clothes and rushed from her apartment. Snowflakes had been falling in a desultory manner since early afternoon, but then, it was supposed to snow in Montreal in early December. Any deviant behaviour on the part of the weather would be met with great consternation and massive speculation about global warming by a population inured to climatic hardship.

She decided to leave her aged car parked in the lane behind her apartment building and caught a bus to the Athletics Department on avenue des Pins. It was Friday evening, and there were few students about. The cavernous lobby was half-filled with teachers, and she glanced around until she spotted Manon Lachance.

"It's not a bad turn-out, is it?" Harry whispered after they had kissed each other's cheeks in the French fashion.

Manon shrugged. "This is the boring part," she said in a low voice as the Dean of Arts and Sciences droned on. "At least there'll be wine and cheese after he's finished, and then we get to party for the rest of the weekend. Thank God for that; these conventions are so boring that I would almost rather teach."

Harry always felt like a giant when she was standing next to Manon. Harry was tall and, over the years, had put on a fair amount of weight, while Manon was diminutive, with curly brown hair and brown eyes, and was as thin as the day she had graduated from university.

"Where's Sue?" Harry asked, referring to Sue Phillips, Manon's lover and also a physical-education teacher. Sue and Manon had been together since university, although their relationship had gone through more bad times than good. Sue was quick-tempered, but everyone knew that most of their problems were Manon's fault. When they periodically broke up, Manon moved in with other women, while Sue withdrew from circulation and lived by herself. Manon's flirtations sometimes led to wretched excess, and although Sue was willing to put up with a certain amount of straying on Manon's part, there were lines which Manon agreed not to cross. But cross them she did and, whenever that happened, Sue walked out. Harry and her ex-girlfriend Judy Johnson had often made up the sofa-bed late at night for a tight-lipped and obviously distraught Sue. But Manon and Sue had been together for the past five years, so Harry hoped that Manon was finally settling down for good.

Manon shrugged her bony shoulders. "She dropped me off and then went to look for somewhere to park the car. I told her that we should put it in the garage for the winter and take the Métro, but no, she said it was too bloody cold. Well, what does she expect? It's always cold in the winter. Me, I would rather shiver a little on a subway platform than drive around in circles, looking for a place to park."

"*C'est vrai*," Harry agreed. "You're right."

"I must have listened to a speech like this a hundred times before," Manon complained. "Why don't we get out of here as soon as Sue gets here? We could go to the bar and get the weekend off to a good start."

"But I thought everyone was going to meet here first," protested Harry.

"They'll find us at the bar." Manon laughed. "And no one will even notice that we've gone."

Before Harry had the chance to reply, Sue Phillips rushed in. She gave Manon a brusque peck on the corner of her mouth, then turned to Harry and bussed her once on each cheek. She smelled as fresh as the wintry outdoors. Sue was a little taller than Manon, with wavy, shoulder-length auburn hair, milky skin and green eyes.

"Did I miss much?" she asked, slipping her arm through Manon's.

Manon snorted but said nothing. The dean seemed to be winding down, or perhaps his voice was giving out. It didn't matter much, since no one appeared to be listening. Harry nodded at several physical-education teachers she knew. The majority of them were scattered in small groups throughout the room.

Sue gave Manon a nudge. "There's Julie," she said, pointing at a tall, svelte woman with long, blond hair. "I wonder where Francine is?" Francine was Manon's twin sister and Julie's lover.

Julie Beliveau took pride in her physical appearance. Of the whole pack of them, she was probably the only one who could keep up with, if not actually outdo, her students. She had been one of the first people Harry knew to join a fitness club, and she still worked out and lifted weights four or five times a week.

"Francine wouldn't come to something like this," Manon scoffed. "Besides, she has to work at the bar later tonight. She's probably sleeping or parked in front of the TV. Same difference, actually."

Desultory applause startled Harry. The dean had stopped speaking. Harry clapped enthusiastically, watching Julie Beliveau saunter across the room in her usual sultry way. It was as if she was smouldering inside and wanted everyone to know it. Harry had never been able to figure out whether it was a conscious or unconscious gesture, but it didn't matter. The end result was the same; women were forever cruising Julie, much to Francine's annoyance. There was enough of the old-time butch in Francine for her to be acutely jealous, but Julie didn't seem to care, even though they had been together for five years. Harry didn't know whether there was any hanky-panky going on behind the scenes, but she wouldn't have been the least bit surprised if there was.

The applause died down and white-jacketed waiters carrying trays filled with glasses of champagne began moving through the crowd. Manon snared two glasses, one for herself and a second for Sue, but Harry gestured her refusal. She was reluctant to have a drink on an empty stomach, especially champagne.

Harry watched Julie Beliveau put an arm around Margaret Alexander. Marg had studied physical education at McGill but had moved to Toronto a few years after graduation. Since most of her family had stayed in Montreal, she returned often over the years and kept in touch with several members of the old crowd. Earlier in the week, Marg had told Harry that she was being encouraged to take early retirement because of her worsening arthritis. While many teachers her age were ready to give up working, she wasn't. She was bitter that pressure was being put on her to stop teaching, even though she found it increasingly difficult to do a good job training her students, especially in the gym.

A flush spread across Marg's face as Julie steered her toward Harry, Manon and Sue. Harry wondered what Julie had said to provoke Marg. It must have been a zinger, because Marg, who had curly black hair and piercing blue eyes which gleamed with intelligence, was rarely rattled. Then again, Julie could be diabolic at times, while writing it off to playfulness.

Harry reached out her hands, which Marg grasped. "It's good to see you again. I'm so glad that you managed to come."

"As I said the other day, Toronto's not all that far away." Marg gave Harry's hands a slight squeeze before releasing them. "I haven't been paying close attention to the conference because I'll likely be retiring after this year. Anyway, too much theory clogs the mind. I've seen student teachers simply paralyzed with the inability to decide which textbook solution to use on a problem in the classroom, or how to put theory into practice. But it's a good excuse to see some of my friends."

"I know what you mean," Harry said with a sympathetic nod. Once she stopped teaching, would she ever again attend a teachers' convention?

"Where have you been hiding yourself?" Julie interjected, hugging Harry for such a long time that Harry's skin began to tingle, even though she was still wearing her bulky leather jacket.

"I've been hard at work, as usual," responded Harry.

"That's not what I heard. Rumour has it that you've holed up in your apartment with some sexy young lady from out west."

Harry gave an awkward laugh. "That's a particularly erroneous rumour, then."

"Don't lie to me, now," Julie said with a shake of her finger. Her nails were coated with bright red nail polish.

"Have you ever known me to evade the truth?" Harry bantered, although she was uncomfortable with Julie's insinuations. She had little patience with innuendo, especially when it was used to demoralize or embarrass.

"Do you mean to tell me that there's no young thing lurking under your covers?" Julie demanded.

"Apparently there was, but Harry left her in San Francisco," interjected Manon.

"So it's true, then. How clichéd; you left your heart in San Francisco," remarked Julie, ignoring Manon's groan. "Tell me everything."

"What's to tell?" Harry gave Manon a dirty look. She should have known better than to confide in someone who had never been particularly closed-mouthed about anything. Now everyone in their circle of friends and acquaintances would find out about Raven Stone, the young punk lesbian with whom she had become lovers while vacationing in San Francisco last June. Not that she minded people knowing. Actually, maybe she did mind, Harry admitted to herself. Taking a young punk as her lover was one thing in San Francisco, where no one knew her, and another thing entirely in Montreal, where too many people knew her all too well.

"*Bon.* Stop making faces at me, *chérie.* After all, you didn't tell me not to say anything," Manon said to Harry. Her tone was plaintive, as if she was the wounded party.

"Never mind." Harry tried to keep her equilibrium. She knew that the more upset she got, the more theatrical Julie's performance would become.

A knowing smile curved the corners of Julie's lips. "You surprise me, Harry. After all those years you lived with Judy, I was certain that you would mope for months, if not forever. I never imagined that you would find someone else so quickly, not with a personality like yours."

What did she mean, a personality like hers? Harry knew that her friends thought she was a quiet sort, a home-body, a nice, dependable woman. Little did they realize, she thought wryly. Shortly after Harry inherited the guesthouse, Judy Johnson, her lover of twelve years, left her for a close friend, Sarah Reid. Harry met Raven a few months later, and although the sexual attraction between them was immediate and strong, it was too soon after her break-up with Judy for her to commit herself. But Harry had stayed in San Francisco, moved into Raven's apartment and remained there for nearly three months, until early September. During that time she fell in love, but there were problems with their relationship, not the least that Raven was twenty-five and Harry was fifty. Toward the end of August, Harry told Raven that she was going to return to Montreal to teach for a final term while deciding what she wanted to do with the rest of her life.

Manon looked out of sorts. She put her empty champagne glass on the tray of a passing waiter and said, "Come on, Julie — who cares about Harry's mysterious girlfriend? Let's get out of here."

"*I* care about Harry's mysterious girlfriend," Julie asserted. "And I'm perfectly willing to wait until later to hear all about her. But I know that our party girl here would rather hang out at the bar."

"Oh, shut up," muttered Manon.

"You know it's true — you've always loved to party," Julie insisted, wagging her finger in Manon's direction. "Anyway, go to the bar if you like. But wait until you hear what I have to suggest before you make up your mind. You're all invited back to our place for something to eat, although it will be out of a box."

"But we just ate," protested Manon.

"So what? A little beer and pizza never hurt anyone. Francine will be there for the first part of the evening, until she has to go to work. She'll be all ears, too. Besides, you'll be hungry before long," Julie said.

"What do you mean?" asked Sue.

"I'm challenging you to a quick game of ball before we go," Julie said.

"*What?*" Manon exclaimed.

Sue gave Julie a dirty look, and then said, "If I'm not mistaken, she's referring to basketball."

Marg chuckled. "What other kind of ball is there?"

"Do you really have to ask?" asked Julie. "Come on, let's have a game for old time's sake."

Sue rolled her eyes.

"Don't be silly," Harry retorted. "We haven't got the right clothes on and we're all wearing boots."

"So we'll play in our socks. What, aren't yours clean? Or are they full of holes? Or — miracle upon miracle — are you afraid to play me?" Julie gloated.

They stared at her.

"Let's do it," Manon said seconds later, a cunning grin on her face.

Oh, what the hell, Harry thought. Why not? "There are only five of us, so we'll need one more person."

"No, two more people," Marg interjected. "I would love to show you how the game should be played, but I can't afford to aggravate my arthritis."

An unsuspecting out-of-towner from Quebec City named Sophie Lister was recruited, not because she possessed any special skills, but because they knew her and she happened to be standing nearby. Julie easily charmed her into agreeing to join them. Then they convinced another physical-education teacher, Elizabeth Martin, that playing ball after a champagne reception was just the thing to do. Liz, who was very much a loner, was one of Manon's ex-lovers. They had gone out in college, although, according to Manon, it had just been a passing fancy. Manon had confided to Harry that not only did Liz have brown eyes, brown hair and a preference for brown clothes, she also had a brown personality. While Harry had outwardly scolded Manon for her snide comment, she had inwardly agreed. Liz could bore even the most patient listener.

Because of the reception, the gym was accessible, the locker room open. The only problem was that they didn't have a basketball. Harry hoped that this would prevent Julie's insane challenge from being played out. Unfortunately, the blue-eyed Marg Alexander exhibited a surprising talent by picking the lock to the supply cupboard, where basketballs abounded.

"I used to do this all the time," she confided to Harry as she plucked two balls from the cupboard and closed the door.

"Whatever for?"

"Oh, once in a while some of us would decide to have a pick-up game in the middle of the night, so we would sneak out of residence and into the gym," Marg responded.

Harry wondered how she had missed these extra-curricular activities, then remembered that she had been completely preoccupied with Barbara Fenton. While the others had been going one-on-one in the gym, she and Barb had been doing the same thing in bed.

"So this is nothing new, then."

"Not really," Marg replied. "We used to gloat about being so smart, getting into the gym like that. But now that I think back, I'll bet the profs knew exactly what we were doing. I mean, how could they fail to notice that the gym lights were on?"

Harry laughed. "It's not as if the gym is some tiny room without any exterior windows, either."

"But they let us go ahead," Marg mused. "These days, we'd be surrounded by security guards if we tried to pull a stunt like that. Times have certainly changed, haven't they? Anyway, let's take these balls back to the gym before Julie comes looking for us."

And so, less than ten minutes after Julie Beliveau had challenged the rest of them to a pick-up basketball game, their winter coats were hanging in lockers and their salt-stained boots were scattered throughout the locker room. No one disputed that Julie would be the captain of one team and that Manon would lead the other. Harry was relieved that Manon picked her first, but Sue, a skilled offensive basketball player, went to Julie. Then Manon took Liz, who had always been a good defensive player. Sophie, the out-of-towner, went last, since no one could remember what she was good at, if anything.

Harry joined Manon and Liz on the sidelines.

"You're all overdressed," Marg said. She sat down on one of the bleachers and smirked at the expression on Harry's face.

"She's right," Manon agreed. She removed her sweater and lowered her pants.

Liz began stripping.

Great, Harry thought, feeling totally outclassed. Manon was wearing a matching sports bra and tights, and Liz was dressed in a white tee-shirt and black underwear. Her midriff was washboard stiff. How could Harry have known when she put on her clothes that morning that she was going to be playing basketball in her skivvies? She groaned mentally when she recalled that she had on her oldest — and least favourite — pair of panties, although her sports bra was relatively new. That would teach her to neglect her laundry until her clothes hamper overflowed. She removed her jacket and blouse but left her suit pants on; they would probably be ruined by the end of the game, but she wasn't about to expose her tatty underwear and be teased about split seams and missing segments of elastic.

Harry glanced across the floor at the women on the other side of the gym, relieved to see that Julie was the only member of the opposing team who had stripped down to the bare essentials, and they were skimpy, indeed. Harry took a deep breath and forced her eyes away from Julie's shapely body. She would never hear the end of it if Julie caught her staring at her. Both Sue and Sophie were still wearing their trousers and Sophie had decided to retain her sweatshirt. Still, if anyone entered the gym now, they would think the whole of lot of them were nuts.

"I'll take Julie," Manon said with a grin. She flexed her biceps and walked onto the floor.

"This is going to be a massacre," Liz groaned.

Harry agreed, but kept her thoughts to herself. If only no one remarked about the rolls of fat around her midriff, she would go on a diet the minute the game ended — if she could manage to walk off the floor at that point.

"I'll take Sophie." Since Sophie was still fully dressed, Harry hoped she would play cautiously to protect her clothes.

In the beginning, Harry thought she had made the right choice. She and Sophie worked up a light sweat running up and down the floor, attempting to outmanoeuvre each other to the ball, but there was no physical contact between them. It looked to Harry like Liz and Sue were also playing carefully, but Manon and Julie were running at full tilt, slapping the ball away from each other and playing a tough, physical game. Although Manon was short and wiry, and Julie tall and muscular, they seemed to be evenly matched, likely because of Manon's phenomenal leaping ability.

Manon one-armed the ball to Harry and shouted, "Get with it, will you? You can play a lot better than that!"

The ball slipped through Harry's fingers and thudded against Sophie's chest, making her wince.

"*Tabernacle!*"

Harry glanced at the dark-eyed Sophie, who looked annoyed. She lunged for the ball just as Sophie moved toward it, and they collided and went down. Harry had forgotten how hard the floor was. She felt winded, but instinctively turned in the ball's direction, scooped it up and threw it to Liz.

"That's better," Manon yelled on the way past.

Liz side-stepped Sue and passed the ball to Manon, who deked, dribbled around Julie and put up a perfect shot which bounced off the backboard and went cleanly through the hoop.

Harry got up, a grin on her face despite the tear in her pants and the ache in her hip. She, Manon and Liz gave each other high-fives, then fell back defensively. This was fun! At least until Julie suddenly headed right at her, the ball thumping in a low dribble. Harry knew that Julie expected her to move aside, but she planted her feet and slapped at the ball as Julie attempted to go around her.

"So you haven't forgotten everything." Julie laughed as she pulled the ball tight against her chest. Her face was flushed with excitement and her hair swirled around her head like a blond halo as she moved. She looked ferocious.

Harry gritted her teeth and lunged. She wrapped her hands around the ball and held on for dear life as Julie backpedalled, trying to dislodge her.

"Jump ball! Jump ball!" Manon screamed.

"Shit!" Julie muttered, letting go so swiftly that Harry staggered.

Why had she bothered? Harry wondered, handing the ball to Marg, who had come on the floor to officiate the jump ball. She had never beat

Julie Beliveau at a jump ball, not even when they had been students and she had been in the best shape of her life.

"Grown a little spare tire, have you?" Julie hissed in a low voice as they jostled for position.

Marg, who was standing beside them and holding the ball, looked shocked. "Don't get insulting."

"Oh, I'm sure old lover girl here can take it," Julie retorted.

Harry pursed her lips but said nothing.

"You never could jump worth beans and, with all that extra weight, I'm surprised you can get off the floor," Julie said, a gleam of amusement in her eyes.

Harry looked at Marg. "What are you waiting for?"

"Not a damn thing." Marg tossed the ball into the air.

As it rose over their heads, Harry gave Julie a quick hip-check, then jumped as high as she could. It wasn't high enough, of course, but her hip-check put Julie off balance just long enough for Harry to slap the ball on its downward path before Julie towered over her.

"Gotcha," Harry shouted, watching the ball spin toward Manon, who snatched it from the air and dribbled toward the basket.

Harry's feet hit the floor with a thud, rattling every bone in her body. Really, she was much too out of shape to be playing hard ball like this.

"Think you're smart, don't you?" Julie jeered.

"Yeah," Harry shot back.

And that was the truth, Harry thought, cheering as she watched Manon deke past Sophie and go up for the basket.

Harry stood in the shower and let hot water stream over her aching muscles. She had one bruise blossoming on her thigh and another on her upper arm, and a mild sprain of the little finger of her left hand, but she felt great. She, Manon and Liz had won the game. Maybe she should get in better shape and take up softball or tennis. She turned off the water and stepped from the tub onto the thick bathmat. Who was she kidding? she reflected, towelling her body dry. She tended to be a rather sedentary person outside the physical-education classes she taught.

Julie Beliveau had invited everyone who had played in the pick-up game to her house for beer and pizza. But Harry knew from previous experience that Julie was a bad loser, so she decided to dress for power. She put on black jeans, a grey sweatshirt, and a black, short-waisted suede jacket. She tucked her Métro pass and a couple of twenty-dollar bills in the pocket of her jeans, ran a comb through her short, greying hair and left the bedroom. She had just finished switching off all the lights except the one in the hall and had picked up her keys when the telephone rang.

Harry hesitated before answering, then decided that she was being silly. It could be any one of a number of friends, or Pearl Vernon, the woman Harry had hired to run her guesthouse in Key West in her absence, or her parents calling from their retirement home in a coastal village in British Columbia. Or it could be Raven, who wanted her to move permanently to San Francisco. Living in such a gay and lesbian mecca was an attractive proposition, but Harry felt drawn to Key West, to its semi-tropical frontier mentality and the concomitant sense of freedom to re-create herself. She also liked the idea of running Isadora's Hideaway instead of leaving it to someone else, even though Pearl Vernon had proved to be an efficient manager. But Raven felt betrayed when Harry told her that she had decided to move to Key West; Raven didn't understand that, by choosing Key West, Harry wasn't rejecting her. To be truthful, Harry supposed she would react the same way were she in a similar situation.

The phone rang a third time. She picked it up before the answering machine kicked in.

It was Raven.

"So how is your convention?"

"The official sessions are nearly over. But the weekend is full of social events." Harry stared at herself in the hall mirror. She pushed her hairlick flat against her head and held her hand over it. It didn't do much good; the moment she released it, it popped back up. She had threatened more than once to cut those rebellious locks right down to her skull, but she never had the nerve to carry through with it, because she wasn't certain how much of a bald spot it would leave. What if it never grew back? Would she have to shave her head? "But I did play a wicked game of pick-up basketball earlier this evening."

"*You?*"

"O ye of little faith," Harry retorted lightly, although she was, in fact, annoyed.

"Sorry."

"I guess you had to be there."

"I didn't mean to insult you. Let's start over again. Pretend I didn't say that."

Harry dropped her keys on the table. "It's all right."

"No, it's not." Raven sighed. "I know you better than that. I apologize."

"Accepted."

"I love you too," Raven murmured.

The telephone cord was stuck behind the hall radiator. Harry yanked it free.

"Are you having a good time?"

"Yes," Harry said. And it was true. It was likely her last opportunity to see many of her friends before she headed south. She knew that she would keep in touch with some of them, but others she would be unlikely to run into when she visited Montreal. And she had met a lot of them before Raven was even born. There it was again — another judgmental thought about Raven's age.

She carried the phone to the easy chair in the bay window and sat down. The snow had stopped falling, but the wind had picked up.

"I wish you could come down for a visit," said Raven.

Harry had flown to San Francisco for a long weekend in October, and Raven had pressured her to return for American Thanksgiving. But by then Harry had been preoccupied with packing. The end result was that they had seen each other only once since Harry returned to Montreal at the end of August.

"I miss you, too. But we've been through this before. I can't just fly to San Francisco. I've got too much to do. Maybe you could fly down to Key West in January."

"But I don't like not seeing you for such a long time," Raven protested.

Perhaps she was being selfish, but Harry was growing impatient with Raven. It was true that their relationship would remain in a state of inertia as long as they were thousands of miles apart. Perhaps it was her age, or maybe her failed relationship with Judy had left her hesitant, cautious, less of a romantic. Whatever the reason, Harry was not as eager to be in love as Raven was.

"We've talked about this before, Raven, and I can't see any point in getting into it again. There's a lot going on in my life right now —"

"And I would like to be part of it."

"Believe me, you are. I think about you all the time," Harry responded. "But everything is completely upside down at the moment. I have to teach every day, and I'm getting ready to move. I told you before I left that I needed to be by myself for a while."

"Have you been seeing Judy again?"

What a dumb question, and yet so indicative of Raven's inability to understand. "No. I haven't seen her since I came back. I've been teaching during the day, and packing at night and on weekends."

There was a long silence, during which Harry resolved that she wasn't going to feel guilty. Or at least any more than she already did. "Listen, I've got to go. We'll speak soon."

Raven hung up without saying goodbye.

Harry listened to the dial tone for a moment, then put down the phone. She was depressed. Unfortunately, their telephone conversations usually made her feel that way. When they first met, she and Raven had been incredibly attracted to each other. And nothing had changed; Harry still cared about her very much. But her three-day visit in October had been difficult. A needy Raven had tried to cram two months' worth of emotional closeness into one weekend, exhausting them both. As a result, Harry had been as relieved as she was sad when she had hugged Raven goodbye and rushed to the airport for her flight back to Montreal.

Harry got up and walked through the apartment to the kitchen, where she foraged in the fridge freezer until she found an ice-cube tray. She put two ice cubes in a tall glass, poured diet cola into it and carried it back into the living room with her. She nudged her favourite easy chair with her knee until it faced the bay window, and plopped down in it.

Harry lived in a renovated triplex on avenue de l'Esplanade, which was within walking distance of the city's major attractions, at least during the summer. Her second-floor apartment was of the type cleverly called a "shotgun" flat. Each apartment in the block of long, narrow row houses was constructed along a central hallway that reached from the front door to the back balcony. This arrangement had given life to the notion that someone could fire a shotgun through the open front door and hit some poor, unsuspecting individual standing in the backyard. Harry had never heard of anyone successfully accomplishing this feat, but that didn't mean that it hadn't happened.

Harry's apartment was across the street from Fletcher's Field, better known these days as Parc Jeanne-Mance, and several City of Montreal tennis courts. Every spring, she vowed to make liberal use of the tennis courts, but she never again thought about her resolution over the ensuing summer. As well as being a park where families picnicked and people carrying pooper-scoopers walked their dogs while cruising other pet owners, Fletcher's Field also contained several soccer and softball fields. From the bay window of her living room, Harry could see the park and the snow-covered slopes of Mont-Royal, the mountain that bisected the city of Montreal.

She took a sip of diet cola and gazed out the window. The phone rang again. Harry stared at it for a moment before she picked it up.

"Hey, Harry, did you fall asleep in the shower, or what?" It was Manon, her voice booming on the other end of the line.

Harry laughed. "I'm on my way."

"I'll save you a piece of pizza."

"There had better be more than one," Harry declared. "I'm starving."

"*Ciao, chérie.*"

Manon's call spurred Harry into action. There was no point sitting there and feeling sorry for herself. She rose from the chair, pulled on her leather jacket, her woollen hat, scarf and gloves, plucked her keys from the hall table and left, locking the front door behind her. It was snowing again. Harry momentarily considered driving to Julie's, but decided to walk. It wasn't all that far, and a good walk would take the stiffness from her muscles.

Julie Beliveau and Francine Lachance lived in the top unit of one of the large, stately triplexes on the tree-lined boulevard St-Joseph. Julie had purchased the building shortly after she had graduated from McGill. It had been in terrible shape, and she had got it for next to nothing from a grateful owner who wanted to get his money out rather than fix the place up. Julie spent tens of thousands of dollars renovating the triplex. She had rented two of the large flats, and a smaller apartment in the basement, and moved into the third-floor unit herself. The spacious, high-ceilinged apartment looked like a million dollars, and even in Montreal's depressed real estate market, the building itself was worth nearly half that.

Not that Julie wanted to sell, far from it. She was so protective of her home that some of her lovers had never been asked to help rearrange the furniture, much less to move in. Even when they were invited to cohabit, they were encouraged to leave most of their possessions behind. There was room for only one interior decorator, and that was Julie. She treated lovers like guests in her home, there on sufferance only.

Or at least until Francine Lachance came along. Shortly after they became lovers, Francine decamped from her one-bedroom, cold-water, east-end flat and relocated to Julie's. Everyone was shocked, when, less than six months later, Julie made Francine the legal co-owner of her boulevard St-Joseph property. Even Manon didn't know why Julie came to trust her rough-edged twin sister after such a short period of time. Julie must have seen something in Francine the rest of them didn't, although five years later it still wasn't evident to anyone other than Julie what that special something was. Privately, Harry thought that Julie's willingness to risk her future financial security said a hell of a lot more about her real feelings for Francine than her flirtatious conduct with other women.

Harry bounded up the curved outside staircase and rang the doorbell. The door was ajar, so she hurried up the interior staircase and burst through the open door into the foyer.

From the number of boots piled on the tray, it was clear that there were more women there than had played in their pick-up basketball game. Julie had likely invited everyone within shouting distance, and then some.

After removing her books and tossing her coat over the coat tree, Harry walked along the hall to the living room. Manon Lachance and Sue Phillips were standing just inside the door, talking quietly. Sue had obviously gone home before coming to Julie and Francine's. She was dressed in a black track suit with trim that was nearly the colour of her auburn hair. Marg Alexander and Julie Beliveau were sitting on one of the leather sofas. Marg looked grumpy, perhaps because Julie was ignoring her.

Julie was leafing through what appeared to be a thick fashion magazine. She dropped the magazine on the sofa as Harry entered the room.

"Our hero arriveth," she cried, giving a mock swoon as she leaped from the sofa. She was wearing a long, slinky caftan which accentuated her firm but very feminine shape.

Marg lowered her beer bottle and rolled her eyes.

"Never mind," said Manon. "She says that to everybody, don't you, Julie?"

"Don't you believe her, Harry," Julie cajoled.

But Harry wasn't about to get involved in their perpetual bickering. "So where's the pizza?"

"In the kitchen, where else?" Julie responded, approaching Harry and running her fingers through Harry's short hair. Her hand was cold.

Harry stood her ground, although her first impulse was to back up. What had she done to deserve this? Was Julie just goading her, or had winning one lousy jump ball in a pick-up game of basketball made her attractive in Julie's eyes? Had she known that was a definite turn-on, she would have perfected her leaping technique at university, when she had been desperate for a date.

"Come on, I'll show you the way," Julie said.

Julie knew as well as Harry that she didn't need to be directed to the kitchen; she had been at their place a dozen times before. But Julie had a vise-like grip on her upper arm, and she was obviously intent on escorting Harry from the living room.

"Have a good time!" Manon shouted after her. "Don't forget to write!"

"Oh, shut up!" Harry retorted over her shoulder.

Harry heard Manon laugh. Julie pulled her down the hall and into the dining room.

"I know where the kitchen is," she finally protested.

"What am I thinking about? Of course you do," Julie answered smoothly, releasing her arm, although she didn't move away. "Actually I have to confess that I just wanted to get you alone. So tell me, is it true that you're having an affair with a woman half your age?"

Everyone who knew was titillated by the thought that Harry, after the end of a twelve-year, relatively stable relationship, had swiftly become lovers with a veritable youngster.

"Yes," Harry said, perversely gratified, despite her annoyance.

"Well, aren't you something?" Julie purred, shifting her weight from one foot to the other. She hadn't seemed to move closer, but suddenly her body came in contact with Harry's. When Harry tried to move, the back of her thighs collided with the edge of the dining-room table. Meanwhile, Julie's hand slithered along her flank.

What a vulture, Harry thought. She tried to step sideways, which resulted in Julie's hand drifting across her lower belly.

"Don't," she whispered.

"Don't what? I always thought you were more interesting than you appear to be."

Why these backhanded compliments? Harry sucked in her stomach, but the palm of Julie's hand followed.

"Isn't this a cosy sight!" remarked Julie's partner, Francine Lachance. She had slipped into the dining room so quietly that neither Harry nor Julie had noticed. Francine resembled her twin sister except that her hair was shorter and she was a bit heavier. But even though the twins were alike and both of them were lesbians, no one who looked at them for more than a second or two would mistake one for the other. Manon was outgoing, the life of the party, and generally had a cheerful expression on her face, while Francine trusted no one. Years of working as a bartender in a succession of lesbian bars had left her tough and cynical. She bragged that she had seen everything, and Harry tended to believe her without wanting to hear many of the details. Fortunately, Francine wasn't inclined to supply them, except on those rare occasions when she had had too much to drink.

Julie gracefully slid away, leaving Harry exposed to Francine's glare.

What a bitch, Harry thought, giving Julie her best scowl. Not only a bitch, but a cowardly slimeball. Harry watched Julie disappear down the hall to the kitchen.

Harry turned. "Listen, Francine —"

"*Merde!* I've had enough of this bullshit." Francine sounded tired and just a little bitter. "What are you doing, coming on to my woman like that?"

"I wasn't doing a damn thing," retorted Harry.

"*Eh, oui?* Give me a break!" Francine's tone was sardonic.

"*Eh, oui* is right, " Harry insisted. "And you should know better."

Francine's tough demeanor took Harry's breath away, especially in comparison with the easygoing personality of her twin sister, Manon. Harry wasn't reluctant to go one-on-one against Manon on any field of play, but Francine was another matter altogether. There was something primordial about Francine, something uncompromising, impenetrable, and, yes, vicious. Harry wouldn't have been a bit surprised if that was the basis of Julie's attraction to her, at least initially.

Francine tilted her head and inspected Harry from head to toe. "Hey, what am I getting all worked up about? You're not really a threat, are you?"

Harry shook her head rapidly. "No, no. Not in the least. Believe me."

But it was clear from the expression on Francine's face that she wasn't certain. Francine's thick fingers tugged on the thin leather belt threaded through the loops on her jeans, and then settled on her hips.

What was this? The showdown at the OK Corral? A surfeit of nerves made Harry feel like laughing. Since she surmised that her life would be in danger should she so much as titter, she zealously resisted the urge.

Astonishingly, Francine blinked first. She lifted her arm and glanced at her watch. "Aw, hell, I've got to get to work."

"Maybe I'll see you later," Harry said, attempting to be polite. Much to her chagrin, she sounded ingratiating.

Francine eyed her with open suspicion. "Why would you want to do that?"

There was that. Harry moved out of the way as Francine walked toward the front door. Manon was on her way to the kitchen, and the twins high-fived each other as they passed in the hall.

"You been biting on my sister, lady?" Manon joked.

"You've got to be kidding."

"Yeah, I guess," Manon responded. "Especially the way she bites back." She put her arm around Harry's shoulder and pulled her toward the kitchen. "Time for something to eat."

Harry resisted. "I'd rather not."

"I thought you were hungry."

"So's Julie, and not for pizza," Harry confided in a low voice.

Manon roared with laughter.

"It's not funny."

"Don't be such a wimp. Julie's come on to every woman she's ever met, at one time or another," Manon remarked. "You just have to know how to handle her."

Julie poked her head around the corner. "Harry! If you don't hurry up, there won't be anything left to eat."

"Come on, don't let her psych you out," Manon said, giving Harry a push. "Act like a woman and get in there!"

"Well, I did miss dinner tonight, and I am kind of hungry," Harry admitted, turning toward the kitchen. In fact, she was starving. Julie was leaning against the doorjamb and winked at Harry as she passed by. Much to Harry's relief, there were other people in the kitchen. She waved at the dark-eyed Sophie Lister, who had changed from her ripped pants into a black track suit. Sophie was talking with Elizabeth Martin and a couple of male teachers whose names Harry had forgotten. The table was covered with empty pizza boxes, and Harry hurriedly took a paper plate and grabbed a large piece of all-dressed pizza. She carried her plate to the counter and put it down for a moment to pour herself a glass of diet cola.

Isabelle, the youngest and only heterosexual Lachance sister, walked into the kitchen, followed by her husband, Albert Dack.

"*Bonsoir*," Harry said, taking a bite of pizza. It was luke-warm, but she was so hungry that she didn't care. Isabelle strongly resembled Manon and Francine, but she was stockier than either of them. She was three years younger than the twins, and she had initially followed in her sisters' footsteps by registering in physical education at McGill. But for reasons Harry had never learned, she had soon switched to primary education and taught grade school throughout her career.

"Harry, *comment ça va?*" Isabelle asked. "How are you?"

Harry washed down a mouthful of pizza with some diet cola, and replied, "Just fine. And you, Albert?"

Albert was hovering near his wife. He was a tall, cavernous, slightly stooped and rather taciturn man. Harry couldn't imagine how he held the attention of a class of high-school students, although she knew that he had taught literature at the same school throughout his career. He usually accompanied Isabelle when she visited Manon and Sue or Francine and Julie. This puzzled Harry; Albert certainly didn't seem overly fond of his two lesbian sisters-in-law or their partners. In fact, he didn't seem to like gay people in general. Harry wondered whether he doggedly followed his wife to family events because he was determined to keep an eye on her. If Harry had been a spiteful person, she likely would have wished that Albert's worst fears would come true, that some horny dyke would try to seduce Isabelle. But then, she wasn't a spiteful person.

"I'm fine," Albert replied, his eyes sliding away from Harry and fastening on the empty coffee pot.

"Albert's a bit preoccupied. He's got to finish grading a whole stack of papers this weekend," Isabelle explained.

Harry stuffed pizza into her mouth. "I think I'll take another piece before it's all gone."

"The pizza's cold, though," said Albert. "Francine should have put it on her heat tray."

"But it wouldn't have all fit," Isabelle said.

Albert frowned. "She could have stacked it."

"I'm not sure that would have worked," replied Isabelle.

Neither was Harry. With visions of a foot-high pile of pizza fused together, with cheese oozing down onto the heat tray and burning to a crisp on its hot surface, Harry excused herself, returned to the table and snatched the last remaining — and cold — slice of pizza.

The next morning, Harry stood in line outside the bus to the Laurentians. In the past, she had avoided most of the social events that were part of the teachers' convention because she wasn't overly fond of organized group activities. But when she had filled out her registration form, she had decided to attend all of them since this was likely her last convention.

She mounted the stairs and looked down the length of the bus. It was packed. Perhaps she should have looked for a place on one of the others.

Julie Beliveau was in the seat just behind the driver, and would have a good view during the trip. "Join me," Julie suggested, patting the spot beside her. Although it was a bitterly cold day, Julie was the first person Harry had seen wearing a coat made of real fur. It was well cut and obviously expensive, with a wide collar that rode high on her neck. Julie had an inviting expression on her face, but Harry demurred. She wasn't all that eager to get close to her, especially after the way Julie had come on to her last night.

"I promised Sue that I would sit with her, so I had better see whether there's space," Harry fibbed, faking a regretful shrug.

"Perhaps on the way home, then," responded Julie, not looking the least bit perturbed.

Harry hurried down the aisle, looking for Sue. Unfortunately, she was sitting at the back of the bus. Harry, who tended toward car sickness when she wasn't driving, hated sitting at the back of the bus, since it wiggled like the tail of a fish. She sighed and plopped down beside Sue, who had her auburn hair pulled back in a ponytail. This accentuated her pale skin, which was covered with freckles, even though it was winter.

"Where's Manon?"

"She driving up to Mont-Tremblant," replied Sue.

Harry was surprised; after all, just last night Manon had been talking about putting their car up on blocks for the rest of the winter, and now she was driving it on the highway instead of taking the bus. Among other things, this seemed rather antisocial. "How come?"

"Oh, she hates going anywhere on a bus," Sue said with a shrug. "She says that it reminds her of those compulsory field trips she took as a student. If she gets bored, she can't leave, and you know her — she's got a rather short attention span. She gets restless pretty fast if she's not having a good time."

"And you didn't want to go with her?"

"I was going to, but we had an argument this morning."

"Oh."

"Don't get me wrong. It was nothing much."

Like hell, Harry thought. "Come on, Phillips, you never could lie."

Sue laughed and then relaxed. "Much to my eternal downfall, it seems. We were bickering in that old, familiar way couples do when they've been in a relationship for a long time. You must know what that's like. Manon wasn't in a very good mood, and I didn't feel like pampering her. I knew if I drove up with her, I'd lose my temper before we got out of the city and we would be having a full-fledged argument by the time we got there."

Harry didn't ask what Manon and Sue had been quarrelling about. It probably didn't matter. Sometimes couples argued for the sake of arguing, and not for much else. She looked out the window as the bus driver backed up, then exited the bus station. Twenty minutes later, he was bullying his way through dense traffic on the Decarie, a north-south expressway that gouged through the west end of the city. She grimaced as he rounded the curve to the exit for the Laurentian autoroute and took the crowded ramp at much too high a speed.

"Cowboy," Sue muttered.

Harry grinned and put on sunglasses to protect her eyes from the glare of the snow. She had always liked Sue Phillips. In contrast to Manon, who often hid her thoughts behind a cheerful demeanor, Sue was straightforward and precise. She had a well-developed sense of what was right, which was likely why she had a quick temper. Or so Harry thought. And being in a relationship with Manon for over two decades hadn't tamed Sue's tempestuous nature.

The bus fishtailed as it slid over a patch of black ice, and Harry's stomach lurched. "I've got to sit somewhere else before I lose my breakfast," she told Sue, who gave her a sympathetic nod. Harry got up and walked toward the front of the bus, but there wasn't an empty seat with the exception of the one next to Julie.

"Have you finally grown bored with Phillips?" Julie asked, her tone arch.

"I get car sick when I sit in the back," Harry replied.

Julie removed her fur coat from the aisle seat. "I've heard better lines, but join me anyway. And stop looking so timid: I'm not going to bite you."

Harry wasn't so sure about that. But the bus was bouncing over frozen potholes and she was having a hard time keeping her balance, so she sat down. Julie promptly tossed her fur coat over their laps, which made Harry feel so uneasy that she pushed it aside.

Julie leaned back against the window and looked at Harry. Her inspection was both speculative and amused. "You've never really liked me, have you?"

"What makes you think that?"

"Don't be a fool, Harry," scoffed Julie. "We went through university together and I was one of Barb's friends, so I know very well what you're like. You've always been one of those holier-than-thou lesbians who looked down on dykes who play around, but, then, while you were with Judy, I suppose you could afford to be sanctimonious. How long were you together? Ten or twelve years? That's a long time. Anyone could get complacent about how tough it is to survive emotionally out there in the real world. But things have changed, haven't they?"

Harry pursed her lips but said nothing. She had never thought of herself as sanctimonious or holier-than-thou, although perhaps there was some truth in what Julie said. But what business of Julie's was it?

She had heard the rumours about Julie cheating on Francine, and last night she had had a taste of Francine's response to any perceived interest in her girlfriend. Harry thought about how she had reacted when Judy first told her that she was having an affair. She hadn't tried to intimidate Judy's lovers, but she had been shocked, jealous and angry. She had sought out lovers of her own as partial compensation, but, even so, she had never entirely got over those feelings.

"You don't like Francine, either," Julie continued. "Maybe that's because she's tough and lets it show."

"I don't dislike Francine," Harry protested. And that was the truth, although it was clear that Julie didn't believe her. She liked Manon better, but there was no law against that. "It's just that Francine and I don't have much in common." Francine had her own set of friends, as did Julie, while Harry, Judy, Manon and Sue had spent a lot of time together over the years.

"I know — you're Manon and Sue's friend." Julie's voice was filled with scorn. "Of course, Sue's always been the little woman in that family. She rolled over the minute she and Manon met. Manon's always been butchy, just like Francine. Maybe that's why you don't like her."

"Don't be silly." Harry realized she was the one who sounded foolish, but she wasn't willing to follow where Julie was leading.

"You disappoint me," Julie said lightly.

Harry stared at her seatmate as Julie gathered up her fur coat and wrapped it around her, but she didn't say anything.

Her conversation with Julie had left a bad taste in her mouth. What had Julie wanted? Had she expected Harry to confess that she disliked her and her lover? Perhaps she had simply wanted Harry to argue with her. What a strange woman.

The bus driver careened down the autoroute, then thumped the steering wheel. He flicked his turn signal and pulled out, cutting off a dirty, battered-looking van. The driver of the van honked his horn in protest but braked and dropped back. He had better sense than to tangle with a motor vehicle so much larger than his.

As soon as the bus came to a stop in front of the ski chalet, Harry hurried down the steps and into the building. The air was still, but it was several degrees colder than in the city. Even though she was dressed warmly, she was freezing. She stomped her feet and blinked her tearing eyes.

"Finally," Manon said, rushing to meet Harry and Julie. She threw up her hands in gesture of impatience.

"I thought we'd never get here," Julie remarked. "Harry wasn't very good company."

Harry dismissed a momentary sense of annoyance. "I don't know about you, but I'm starving," she said to Manon.

"*Moi aussi,*" Manon agreed with a nod.

They waited for Sue to get off the bus and hurried into the dining room. Rubber chicken it was, in the best ski-chalet style. No one seemed to care. Connoisseurs of good food did not eat in dining areas adjacent to outdoor swimming pools where scantily clad bathers shrieked in response to the extreme temperature difference between the water and the surrounding air. Harry dawdled overlong having a polite chat with two straight teachers, and got separated from Manon, Sue and Julie. She ended up sitting between Liz Martin and Marg Alexander. As she picked at the food on her plate and listened to Liz drone on about staff politics at the school in which she taught, Harry stared out the plate-glass, floor-to-ceiling window past the frolicking bathers. Not far from the chalet, the pristine slopes of the ski hills rose majestically. The bare trees looked grey in the cold winter light. There was a short line-up for the ski lift, and the trails were dotted with skiers.

"Are you going skiing?" Liz asked Harry.

"No, I don't ski." Harry, who had plenty of experience with the response of ski-crazed Quebeckers to this statement, steeled herself for Liz's reaction.

But instead of looking astonished, Liz looked pleased. "Neither do I. Perhaps we can spend the afternoon together in front of the fireplace and reminisce about old times. Remember when Manon and I were dating? We took you under our wings and shepherded you around. I do believe you met Judy at a party we took you to."

Harry had completely forgotten about that. She supposed she should feel indebted to Liz, but it had been such a long time ago. Liz had been crazy about Manon, who had swiftly grown contemptuous of such conspicuous adoration. By the time Harry met Judy, Manon had barely been able to tolerate Liz.

"I'd love to, but Marg and I are going for a little hike," Harry fibbed. She gave the startled-looking Marg a beseeching glance, and Marg rose to the occasion.

"Yes, we decided not to sit around inside on such a beautiful day."

For a moment Harry thought Liz was going to offer to join them, but then she said, "Well, I would like to tag along, but it's too cold out there for me."

"I'm sure lots of other people will feel the same way," Harry said in a soothing voice. Now that she had managed to escape from an afternoon with Liz, she felt guilty.

"Shall we go, then?" Marg asked, getting up from the table. Like Harry, she had left most of her lunch on the plate.

Harry followed Marg from the room. "I wasn't serious," she said quietly.

Marg gave her a shrewd smile. "I was. I don't ski either, but here we are in the country, and it's such a beautiful day. I wouldn't even think of staying inside. Most everyone who is outside will be either skiing or swimming, but I just want to go for a walk."

She had been hoisted with her own petard, Harry thought wryly. She followed Marg to the coat room, where they retrieved their jackets. Harry zipped up hers, firmly pulled her hat down over her ears and wrapped her scarf tightly around her neck.

They went out. The air was crisp, and there wasn't a cloud in the pale winter sky. Harry shivered and put on her sunglasses. Groups of skiers hurried past them on their way to the lift. Marg pointed at a sign. "This trail will take us over that hill."

A narrow, winding trail led up through a fairly dense stand of trees. The top of the hill looked a long way off. Harry shivered again and plunged her gloved hands into the pockets of her leather jacket.

"Come on. You'll warm up once we get moving."

Harry doubted it, but she trudged after Marg. They climbed to the line of trees and, once they entered the woods, all Harry could hear was her heavy breathing and the squeaking noise their boots made in the snow. The trees and the snow muffled all other sound. It was remarkably pristine and peaceful, and before long Harry perked up. Her movements took on a certain rhythm as she marched after Marg, and by the time they broke free of the trees and reached the top of the hill, Harry was not only warm, she was sweating.

Marg brushed the snow off a newly fallen tree in a clearing and sat down.

Harry wasn't an admirer of winter, but the view was impressive. The mountain towered over the ski chalet, which looked like a miniature castle. Wisps of steam rose from the swimming pool. Harry sat down beside Marg and watched skiers snake gracefully down the hill. Perhaps she would feel differently about cold weather if she learned a winter sport. But that was a moot point, since she would soon be residing in the south. Sometimes she had to remind herself that she was leaving Montreal.

"Look, there're Manon and Julie," Harry said, pointing to a ski hill on the side of the mountain.

"How on earth can you tell it's them? They're so far away," asked Marg.

"I recognize their ski jackets," Harry responded. "Manon wears hers whenever it's really cold out."

"I hate winter," said Marg.

She sounded so bitter that Harry turned and looked at her. "What's the matter?"

"Nothing. Everything." Marg pulled a pack of cigarettes from her coat pocket, took one out and lit it with a match.

Harry was shocked. "When did you start smoking?"

"I've always smoked, but only when I'm under stress," Marg replied. "I'm a closet smoker. Please don't tell anyone."

Harry glanced at her to see if she was joking, but she wasn't. "Tell me what's bothering you. It's not just the weather, is it? It might be cold, but, as you said after lunch, here we are in the country, and it's such a beautiful day."

"I hate the way people behave."

"What do you mean?"

"All the chattering and flirting and carrying on."

"Why on earth do you feel like that?"

"Because none of it means anything. Maybe it's fun for you because you live in Montreal, but I moved away so long ago that I never quite fit in when I come back," Marg replied.

"Really?" Harry had always thought that Marg fit in quite well. Everyone liked her. "Then why do you bother?"

"Good question," Marg said with a laugh. "I have a circle of friends in Toronto, but everybody pales eventually, and I get to thinking that the grass is greener here."

But Toronto was a big city, larger than Montreal. And there wasn't the language divide there.

"Maybe you need to get in with a different crowd," Harry suggested.

"Don't you think I know that? But how? All the gay and lesbian groups are filled with young people. Hardly anyone over thirty goes to their events. And you can't meet anyone in the bars."

Although Harry had indeed met Raven in a bar, she knew that what Marg said was essentially true. She also understood how difficult it was to make new friends, much less find a lover. She knew she had been lucky to have become involved with Raven such a short time after Judy. She hadn't experienced that constant tingle of anxiety about being alone, nor had she had to search for someone to fill the hole in her emotional life.

Marg bent over and put out her cigarette in the snow. Then she took off her hat and ran her gloved fingers through her curly black hair. "I've placed ads in the personal columns in the gay and lesbian newspapers in Toronto, but they haven't worked. Not yet, at least. You know, I used to envy you and Judy. Even though I wasn't around a lot, you were like an oasis of sanity in my life, a couple I could look up to. Why did the two of you break up?"

Harry was taken aback by the suddenness of Marg's question. She didn't know what to say. She had never discussed what had happened between her and Judy with her friends, not in any great detail, at least. Should she tell Marg that Judy left her for another woman? That Judy moved out because she wanted a change? That Judy was going through a mid-life crisis and no longer believed in monogamy? That they both had other lovers before they split up? How could she explain that all of that was true?

"Sometimes people fall out of love," she said, knowing it wasn't an adequate response.

"That's it?"

"No, of course not." Love, whether you were falling in or out of it, was never so simple, so cut and dried. Judy had fallen out of love first. Harry had suffered. Other women had suffered. There had been a lot of grief. It had been messy. Actually, it still was. "I won't lie to you, Marg. I thought Judy and I were together for life, but things didn't work out that way. I don't really know why."

Marg frowned. "That's downright depressing."

Isn't it? Harry thought. "Well, I try to look on the bright side of things," she said, even though this wasn't the truth. But her inheritance from Barb had given her the opportunity to start over again. And she was involved with Raven, although the outcome of their relationship wasn't certain.

"Well, I wish you luck. As for me, I'd give almost anything to be able to begin again," Marg said with a sigh. She got up, wiped snow from her behind and stretched. "But never mind. My life isn't all that bad. I still enjoy my work, and my arthritis hasn't flared up lately. It's just that I'm lonely, and at my age it's hard to find someone. And after I retire, it will be even harder to meet people."

But they were the same age, Harry wanted to protest. She stood up and hurried after Marg. "You shouldn't feel so pessimistic. We're not old, after all."

"Yes, yes, I know. I've heard it all before," Marg said impatiently. "You're only as young as you feel, fifty isn't ancient, it's just middle age. Well, let me tell you something, Harriet Hubbley, sometimes I feel *old*. I look around at my peers and see them dieting away middle-age spread, dying the grey out of their hair, getting their teeth whitened and sneaking off for electrolysis to get rid of all those pesky chin hairs. And when they're not sleeping around behind their lovers' backs or dating younger women, all they can talk about is how much pension they're going to get and where they're going to retire. You're not dumb, Harry; what do you think it all means?"

"I don't know," Harry admitted. She felt sorry for Marg, so she struggled to answer. "I don't like the idea of getting older, but we don't have much choice in the matter, do we? So I try not to think about it too much."

"You don't have a chronic disease that reminds you of your mortality," Marg reminded her.

"You're right." Harry tramped through the snow, wondering how she had come to be involved in such a philosophical discussion. She hadn't been evading the issue when she told Marg she didn't think about aging if she could avoid it. She preferred to let it happen, not to analyze it to death. What good did it do to fret about it when she couldn't stop the clock from ticking?

"Everyone rebels against growing old," commented Marg. "Even you, despite your protestations to the contrary."

"What?"

"Why else did you become involved with a woman half your age?"

"Oh, I don't know that being rebellious has anything to do with it," Harry protested. "I mean, why should we 'act our age,' so to speak? After all, we're not like our parents' generation. Why shouldn't we enjoy ourselves? You were there when we played basketball yesterday—even if we're not as fit as we used to be, we still had fun."

"I suppose," Marg said.

But it was clear to Harry that Marg wasn't convinced. Marg was evidently looking for someone with whom she could commiserate, so it wasn't long before she changed the subject.

As they neared the ski chalet, they left the protection of the trees and the wind swooped down on them. Snow began to fall shortly after, and by the time they reached the front door of the chalet, they were both shivering. Harry felt chilled to the bone.

"Where have you two been?" Manon demanded the minute they arrived. She was so agitated that she was literally bouncing up and down on her toes. "We've been ready to leave for nearly fifteen minutes."

"Sorry," Harry said. "We lost track of the time."

"Outdoors?" Julie remarked. "Really, Harry. And with *Marg*, of all people."

"Oh, shut up," Harry said angrily. She had had quite enough of Julie's insinuations. She stalked toward the washroom, completely unaware of the shocked expressions on the faces of the women she had left behind in the lobby.

Harry got off at the avenue du Parc Métro station and took the escalator to the surface. The air was frosty and dry, and the snow crunched under her boots. It hadn't started to snow yet in Montreal, but it was expected that a good foot of it would be dumped on the city by dawn Sunday.

She caught a packed bus going north on avenue du Parc. The bus sped through the ghetto where a large number of McGill students lived in row houses and highrise apartment buildings. Then it looped under the Parc-des-Pins interchange and headed along avenue du Parc where it divided Fletcher's Field from the slopes of Mont-Royal. Harry stood up and tugged on the cord. When the bus driver pulled into the sidewalk, Harry got off the bus at the corner of avenue Mont-Royal and avenue du Parc, a block from her apartment on l'Esplanade.

She considered stopping at the *dépanneur*, or convenience store, just up the street for a few things she needed, but decided against it. She wanted to take a shower before setting out for dinner on rue Prince-Arthur and a night on the town. After the rubber chicken they had been served for lunch, she was looking forward to demolishing a fish or chicken brochette with rice, fried potatoes, and a Greek salad liberally sprinkled with feta cheese. Perhaps a good meal would help lift the slight depression that had descended after her fruitless conversation with Julie on the bus and her dispiriting discussion with Marg on the ski hill.

As Harry crossed the street, the wind stirred and it started to snow again. The sky was overcast but bright with the reflection of the city lights. She reached the stairs to her apartment, and only after she grasped the railing with her gloved hand did she realize that someone was standing on the balcony near her front door. Before she had the opportunity to react, the person moved away from the door and began walking down the stairs.

"Harriet?"

Harry was stunned. It couldn't be.

"Raven?"

"Why didn't you tell me how cold it was up here?"

Raven stumbled into her arms. Even though Harry was bundled up in her leather jacket, she could feel her young lover's body shiver convulsively.

Harry's concern about Raven's condition overcame her astonishment.

"Let's get you inside." She took Raven's suitcase and steered her toward the door, fumbling for her keys in the dark. Her key turned in the lock, and she led Raven into her apartment. She dropped the suitcase on the floor, switched on the hall light and stared at Raven, who was wearing black jeans and a black jean jacket over a thin sweatshirt. A plaid scarf was wrapped around her neck.

"No wonder you're cold."

"Don't scold, Harriet," Raven said through blue-tinged lips. "God, I'd like to wrap myself around this radiator. How in hell do you survive this blasted weather?"

Harry had often asked herself that question on frigid mornings when she had to get up early for work and her car wouldn't start after she had spent fifteen minutes shovelling it out.

"You get used to it," she said. "Why don't you get out of those clothes and take a hot shower? That should warm you up. Meanwhile, I'll make a pot of coffee."

"I'd rather have brandy."

"Brandy it is, then." Harry led Raven toward the bathroom and left her there while she returned to the living room and unearthed a long-forgotten, nearly full bottle of brandy from her depleted liquor cabinet. She took the bottle to the kitchen, hearing the shower running as she passed the bathroom. She quickly wiped the dust from the bottle with a dishcloth and then pried out the cork. Her brandy snifters were packed, so she poured a liberal amount of brandy into a teacup. It was only when she placed the cup on the counter that she realized that her hands were shaking.

"Oh, god," she muttered. She pulled out a chair and sat down at the kitchen table. She had never imagined Raven would fly across the continent and descend upon her like this.

"Is this drink for me?" Raven asked.

Harry turned. "Yes."

"Aren't you going to join me?"

"Not right now."

Raven picked up the teacup and drained it. She had wrapped herself in Harry's terrycloth bathrobe. Her extremely short hair accentuated the fine arch of her eyebrows. Her blue eyes were lined with dark circles. Raven shuddered and put the empty cup on the counter.

"I felt so sad last night. It's hard to get anything meaningful from our conversations when I can't see or touch you."

"Yes, I know."

"I couldn't stand it any longer, so I threw some things in my suitcase, took the subway to the airport and flew standby."

The phone rang. Harry let it. After four rings, the answering machine responded.

Raven poured herself another drink and downed it. The blue tinge disappeared from her lips.

Harry's sense of inertia dissipated. "This is quite a shock," she admitted. When she saw the look on Raven's face, she hastened to say, "I'm really glad to see you, though." Why had she never thought of inviting Raven to Montreal? Lack of imagination, she supposed. Or fear of mixing the two distinct lives she seemed to be living at the moment.

"I know you've still got some social events left at your convention, but you could take me with you," Raven said.

Those big blue eyes were so perceptive that Harry imagined Raven could see inside her head and follow her thought processes. Thank goodness she couldn't; her first thought had been entirely selfish and had involved showing off Raven to her friends.

"I won't embarrass you, if that's what you're thinking," Raven said.

"The idea never occurred to me," Harry said quite truthfully. "Besides, all my friends know about you." And even some of her adversaries, she reflected, although she didn't tell Raven that.

"There's no problem, then, is there?"

"No." Not really. Only Harry hadn't planned on integrating Raven into her Montreal life, which already felt chaotic enough. She had wanted to wait until she was established in Key West before seeing her again. Unfortunately, she had never told Raven that she had had a brief affair with Pearl Vernon, the woman she had hired to run the guesthouse, so there was that to deal with, too.

"What's wrong?"

"Nothing. I was just trying to think what you could wear to dinner."

"I've got some fancy stuff in my suitcase."

"I mean *over* your fancy stuff. It's *cold* out there, and there's a major storm brewing. We're supposed to get a foot of snow overnight."

Raven looked enchanted at the idea, which brought a grin to Harry's face.

"That's better," Raven said, moving toward Harry. "I thought you had forgotten how to smile."

Raven's kiss took Harry's breath away. When Raven's hand slid down inside her sweatshirt, Harry felt like she was going to liquefy. It had been a long time from October to December. They rushed from the kitchen to the bedroom and tumbled to the bed together, flinging their clothes to the floor. Harry's need was ferocious, but no more than Raven's. Harry momentarily broke away, fumbled in the drawer in her bedside table and withdrew gloves and dental dams. They came together urgently, skin on skin, mouths and hands eager to explore. A short time later, Harry moaned and came, collapsing beside Raven.

"You've put on weight," Raven whispered, running her hand from Harry's breast to her groin.

"Have I?"

Raven's fingers moved lower. "It doesn't matter."

At that particular moment, Harry didn't care either.

The phone began ringing again.

"You're a popular lady," Raven remarked breathlessly.

"I'm supposed to be downtown having dinner in a Greek restaurant at this very moment," Harry whispered. To hell with it, she thought, pulling Raven's gloved hand back between her thighs. She felt greedy, as if she would never be entirely satisfied. Dinner could wait. She was hungry for another kind of sustenance.

Some time later, a rather dazed Harry raised her arm and picked up the telephone, which was pealing insistently for the third time since they had started to make love.

It was Sue Phillips, and from the noise in the background Harry surmised that she was in the bar.

"Where *are* you?" Sue shouted.

"I've been busy."

And how, Harry mused as Raven ducked under the cord and snuggled against her.

"We've been trying to call you for hours!"

There was a short silence, then Francine Lachance came on the line, vibrantly cursing in French.

"What's the matter?"

Francine switched to English. "If you're with Julie, I'm going to kill you!"

"What are you talking about? Of course I'm not with Julie!"

Raven sat up. "Who's Julie?"

"Listen, where are you?" Harry asked in French.

"At l'Entr'acte. Where else would I be at this time of night?"

Harry didn't bother say that she had no idea what time it was. "Right."

Sue came back on the line. "Harry, are you sure you're not with Julie?"

"Of course I'm not," Harry reiterated. "My girlfriend, Raven Stone, arrived unexpectedly from San Francisco earlier tonight."

"So that's what you meant when you said you were busy," Sue remarked.

Harry gave a rather embarrassed laugh. "Well, yes. We've been making up for lost time, so to speak."

"You little devil." Sue chortled.

Harry felt ill at ease. "Listen, we'll drop by in a little while."

"I'll tell people you'll be around later. Meanwhile, I'll let Francine know that you're not the guilty party — if there is one," Sue said dryly. "Maybe Julie fell asleep in her car, or something."

"I rather doubt it."

"I know what you mean," Sue replied. "*Ciao*."

Harry hung up.

"So who is this Julie?"

"A woman I know," Harry replied, giving Raven a kiss on the top of her head.

"And?"

"I went to university with her," Harry said. "She's tall, blond and gorgeous, and rumour has it that she sleeps around. She has a very jealous lover."

"Sounds like just your type."

"Don't," Harry said, gently moving Raven's hands away from her breasts. "I promised Sue Phillips that we would show up at the bar, and if you start making love to me, we'll be here for the rest of the night."

"I wouldn't mind."

"Duty calls, however," Harry said lightly. She reached out and switched on the lamp on her bedside table. They stared at each other, their bodies bathed with dim light. There was a shy smile on Raven's face and, not for the first time, Harry was shocked at how young she was. The difference in their ages was so easy to forget when it was dark and they were in each other's arms.

"Are you sure you want me to come with you?" Raven asked as Harry rose from the bed.

"Positive." Harry bent down, picked up the covers from the floor and tossed them on the bed. "You can borrow one of my coats, and I've got plenty of hats and scarves, and even an extra pair of boots. But first I'm going to take a shower."

"That sounds like a great idea."

Harry had to resist Raven's playful urging to make love yet again in the shower. But they were both dressed and ready to leave twenty minutes later. Unfortunately, the storm had fully descended on Montreal. Thick snow was falling and the wind was howling.

"I don't relish driving in this," Harry remarked as she locked the front door. "We had better take the bus."

"It's marvellous," Raven enthused. "But it's so slippery!"

"Haven't you ever seen snow before?"

"No. Not like this. Except for on TV, that is," replied Raven, skidding on the balcony. "And it's not the same at all. It's *cold*, for one thing. And wet. And there's so much of it."

"Hey, don't fall down the steps," warned Harry. She grasped Raven's arm and helped the younger woman negotiate the snow-covered staircase.

"So this is what they mean by 'winter wonderland,'" Raven said, staring in amazement.

Harry paused and looked around, but all she could see was falling snow. Everything was covered with the powdery white stuff. She tried to perceive the storm through Raven's eyes, but couldn't. To urban dwellers, snow meant inconvenience, delays, cars to shovel out, snarled traffic.

"This is so romantic," Raven said, giving Harry an intimate smile.

Harry couldn't help but smile back. She tried to remember if she had ever found snow romantic, but came up empty. "You might not think so if you had to get to work on time during one of these storms."

"I'd play hooky."

Harry laughed and looped her arm through Raven's. "I bet you would at that. Anyway, let's go. We've got a bus to catch."

It was nearly eleven by the time Harry and Raven got to l'Entr'acte, a popular lesbian bar located on rue St-Denis a few blocks north of rue Sherbrooke, one of Montreal's main streets.

They descended the short flight of stairs to the door, which was standing wide open.

"It's going to be hot in here," Harry warned. "There's a tiny patio out back, but it's not used during the winter."

"Obviously."

"Even during the summer, the neighbours complain about the noise if the door is left open. It's a bit of a dive, but it's my favourite bar," Harry added. "I like the songs on the jukebox, and most of the women I know come here. It's crowded, especially on weekends."

"Aren't all gay bars?"

Raven had a point. They paused in the tiny, poster-lined foyer to check their coats and winter gear, and then Harry opened the inner door and led Raven into the bar. As she had predicted, it was hot and crowded, and the air was hazy with cigarette smoke. It rose to the ceiling and hovered like smog over the city on a hot day in the middle of the summer. Dance music blared from the jukebox, and Harry's heart began to pound in time to the beat of the music.

"My friends will likely be in the back, somewhere near the dance floor," Harry said.

"Why don't we get something to drink first?" Raven suggested.

"Beer?"

"Sure."

They walked to the crowded bar. Harry breathed a sigh of relief when she saw that Francine Lachance was at the far end. Her back was to Harry, and she was ringing up orders at the cash register in the corner. Harry slid between two stools and gestured to the other bartender. She ordered two Miller Lites, paid, and handed one of the bottles to Raven.

"Come on."

As they made their way toward the back of the bar, the crowds of women grew denser. L'Entr'acte was a low-ceilinged basement bar which, even at the best of times, reeked of beer and cigarette smoke. Harry pushed through the dense knots of chatting women until they reached the back wall. She placed her untouched bottle of beer on the narrow counter and searched the crowd for faces she knew. She saw Sue Phillips dancing with Marg Alexander and Liz Martin, while the dark-eyed Sophie Lister was sitting on a stool in the back corner, nursing a mug of coffee. She had proved herself to be a competent basketball player during their pick-up basketball game. Although none of them knew much about her except that she was from Quebec City, she had swiftly attached herself to their little group.

"Are your friends here?" Raven asked.

"Yes," Harry replied just as Manon Lachance materialized in front of the crowd separating them from the dance floor.

"What a night!" Manon exclaimed, setting her drink down on the counter.

Raven sidled forward.

Harry suddenly felt diffident. What were her friends going to think? Would they believe that she had gone nuts, getting involved with such a young punk lesbian?

"Er — Raven, this is my old friend, Manon Lachance," Harry said. "Manon, this is Raven Stone."

Manon glanced from Raven to Harry and back again, only this time she took a long look at Raven, who had insisted on dressing in one of her more provocative outfits, black leggings with a black bra covered with a skimpy crocheted singlet. "I want to do you proud," she had said to Harry, who nodded dumbly. Sometimes she was shocked by Raven's choice of clothing, but she didn't tell Raven that.

"So this is the girlfriend you've been talking about," Manon said. "I must admit that I'm enchanted."

Raven looked impressed. "The same here."

"Listen, Manon, what's been going on?" Harry asked. "Phillips called earlier, and she was in a stew. So was Francine."

Manon finally stopped staring at Raven and grinned at Harry. "Francine went nuts because Julie disappeared for a little while after dinner, and Francine figured she was doing something she shouldn't be. Francine's my twin sister, by the way," she interrupted herself to explain to Raven. "Some people think we look alike, but I'm cuter and a lot sexier."

Harry snorted.

"*Mais oui*," Manon protested. "You know it's true, Harry. Anyway, Francine has quite a temper, and when she loses it, it's more than enough to sour the evening for everybody, including her customers."

Raven sipped beer from her bottle, put her arm around Harry and leaned against her side.

Manon paused, studying Raven, and then Harry. She looked baffled and not a little envious. "Anyway, I don't think Julie was gone long enough to be up to anything much. See, we had dinner on Prince-Arthur — they reserved the whole top floor, and we pretty well filled the place. Then the group split up. Some of the more cautious teachers went home after dinner because of the storm, especially those who live on the West Island, the South Shore or Laval. You know how slippery the bridges get when there's a storm. Others took taxis back to the hotel. A lot of us went to put our cars in parking lots so we wouldn't get towed to hell and beyond when the ploughs came out. Some people went for coffee on St-Denis. The rest of us came here, although quite a few people have already gone home. It's been a long day."

Harry was puzzled. "That sounds like a typical Saturday night to me. Why was Francine so upset?"

"She thought you and Julie were off somewhere making out," replied Manon. "Mind you, people straggled in over a period of time, me included — I was moving the car, which Sue insisted on bringing. But Francine was certain that you and Julie were together."

"Why would she think that?" Raven interjected.

Oh, shit. "I don't have any idea." Harry didn't mean to tell an out-and-out lie, but she was flustered.

"Come on, Hubbley — Julie's been coming on to you all weekend," Marg said, plopping down on the stool beside Raven and staring openly at her. Really, if everyone paid her that much attention, Raven was going to start preening.

But Raven had other things on her mind. She looked at Harry, her eyebrows raised. "Is that true?"

Harry opened her mouth and closed it again. Damn that Beliveau woman. "Well, yes. She couldn't resist my charms, you see."

Raven gave her a look but didn't say anything.

Sue left the slightly elevated dance floor and pushed through the crowd until she was standing next to Harry. Her auburn hair was dishevelled and her skin was flushed and sweaty from dancing. She gave Harry a kiss on the cheek, glanced curiously at Raven, and asked, "So what's up?"

"Julie," Manon responded before Harry could get a word in edgewise. "You know how she's been after Harry lately."

This was beginning to get out of hand. "But I didn't do a thing to encourage her," Harry said heatedly.

"So she *is* after you," said Raven.

Harry gave Manon a now-see-what-you've-done glare and turned to Raven, but, before she could speak, Manon moved closer and draped an arm around each of their shoulders. Her face was so close to Harry's that Harry could smell beer on her breath.

"*Écoute, ma petite*," she said to Raven.

"What?" Raven asked.

"She wants you to listen to her," Harry responded, leaving out the translation of "*ma petite*" because she didn't imagine Raven would appreciate being called "little one."

Manon leaned even closer to Raven. "I can assure you that you've got nothing to worry about as far as Harry and Julie Beliveau are concerned."

Hell, the way Manon was looking at Raven, Harry was beginning to worry about *her*.

Raven looked curious. "How do you know?"

"Trust me."

At that point, Sue waded into the fray. "Come on, Manon, you're had too much to drink and you're making a nuisance of yourself."

Manon gave an disconcerted laugh and said, "Aw, Phillips, don't be such a spoilsport. I was just having a little fun."

Elizabeth and Sophie chose that moment to join them. Liz was carrying a beer bottle, and Sophie had a half-full coffee mug in her hand. Manon had released her hold on Harry and Raven's shoulders, but she was standing just a little too close to Raven for comfort. Harry introduced Raven to Liz and Sophie and wished that Manon would get lost.

Manon reached behind Harry and snatched Harry's beer. "I see you're up to your usual tricks, Hubbley, letting perfectly good beer get warm." She took a swig and put the bottle back on the counter. "Thanks for the drink, bud. Come on. Sue. Let's dance."

A slow song was playing on the jukebox, and the dance floor filled swiftly. Harry watched Manon and Sue dance. Sue was talking rapidly to Manon, and, from the look on Manon's face, she wasn't much enjoying what her lover was saying to her.

"Time for another drink." Marg Alexander gave Harry and Raven a smile and wandered toward the front of the bar. Liz looked so disappointed that Harry, who was somewhat distracted by Raven's hand travelling up and down her back, wondered whether Liz was interested in Marg.

"Want to dance?" she asked Raven.

"I thought you'd never ask."

As if Raven was your proverbial wallflower, waiting for someone else to put the moves on her, Harry reflected.

"Some friends you have," Raven remarked once they had claimed a tiny spot on the dance floor.

Harry wasn't certain whether Raven was making a positive or a negative comment, although she suspected the latter was more likely. "We go back a long way, especially Manon and I."

Raven snuggled against Harry, making her heart beat faster. It was amazing how easily she grew aroused when Raven touched her.

"I can see that Manon really likes you," Raven said. "But who is this Julie everyone was talking about?"

"I haven't seen her since we came in," Harry replied. Heat was rising in her groin, and she closed her eyes and held Raven tight, letting the music and her arousal take possession of all her senses.

When the song ended, she opened her eyes and looked around the dance floor. Julie Beliveau was staring at her, an amused expression on her face. Julie broke away from Liz Martin, who looked dazed. Julie must have sucked her in like a hungry boa devouring dinner. Couples straggled from the dance floor as pounding dance music blared from the speakers, but Julie deserted the hapless Liz and headed straight toward Harry and Raven. She was wearing skin-tight blue jeans and a short halter that exposed her trim midriff.

"*Chérie*," Julie gushed. "Where have you been? I've been looking for you all evening."

"Julie," Harry mumbled, relieved when Raven stepped forward and put herself between her and Julie.

"I'm Raven Stone," she said, holding out her hand.

Julie looked at it as if she had never seen one before. "Good for you, darling. But, Harry, you really did rob the cradle, didn't you?"

Raven's hand fell to her side. She threw back her head and gave a curt laugh. "Gosh, I thought Harry said you were classmates. How is that? Did you take several years off and then go back to school?"

Harry had never seen anyone stop Julie Beliveau cold in her tracks. It was wonderful. She turned her back on Julie and began to dance. There was barely room to move, and it was hot. Perspiration ran from her hairline down her neck, but she ignored the heat, the sweat, Julie's scowling retreat, and closed her eyes, letting the music take her. Her body sank into a primal, thoughtless state, the beat moving over her like water over sand. She felt Raven's hands grasp hers and lead them to her lips, and then Raven's hands fastened on her shoulders. She opened her eyes and stared at her lover, feeling passion rise between them.

"Let's take a break," Harry said to Raven, wiping the sweat from her forehead.

They had spent the last two hours on the dance floor, with brief stops at a tiny table near the front of the bar.

"I wouldn't mind another drink," Raven replied.

They joined hands and left the dance floor.

"Me neither, but I think I'll go to the washroom first," Harry said. "Why don't you get me some mineral water and I'll meet you at the table?"

Raven nodded and headed toward the bar.

The restroom was empty, although it reeked of marijuana. Harry went into one of the two stalls and locked the door. She folded over several pieces of toilet paper and wiped the sweat from her face and then absently inspected the latest graffiti.

She heard the door open and waited for someone to enter the second stall, but no one did. She could hear a woman whispering, and then a second, deeper voice interrupted the first. She couldn't make out any individual words, but it was clear that the women were speaking in anger. Both sounded furious.

"Well, screw you too!" one of them exclaimed, and then the washroom door closed with a bang.

Harry abruptly stood up. Had that been her ex-lover Judy? It had been hard to tell over the din of the music, muted though it was once the door was closed. She zipped up her pants and left the cubicle, but the restroom was empty. She washed her hands and tried to compose herself. It probably hadn't been Judy. After all, Judy hated bars. She had always objected when Harry wanted to go to one, maintaining that lesbian bars were dingy, noisy, smoky, crowded, expensive and exploitative.

But even if it had been Judy, what difference did it make? Their relationship had ended eight months ago. Judy was living with another woman, and Harry was dating Raven.

Harry dried her hands and paused to stare at herself in the mirror. Her face was flushed and her eyes were smudged with fatigue. She took a paper towel, wiped her greasy nose, then plucked ineffectually at her unruly hair. Oh, the hell with it. She crumbled the paper towel, tossed it into the overflowing garbage can and went out. She spotted Raven leaning over the bar, methodically counting out change.

"Hello, Harry."

Harry turned and stared at her former lover. Judy didn't look particularly happy, but Harry wasn't certain whether that was because she had had an altercation with Sarah in the women's washroom or because she had run into Harry.

"What are you doing here?" Harry blurted. Judy's familiar face, with its high cheekbones and deep brown eyes, brought back memories Harry would rather have kept buried. And she still blamed Judy for the end of their relationship.

Judy raised her eyebrows. "Is that all you have to say? Besides, it's a free country."

Harry's hands were trembling, so she shoved them into her pants' pockets. "But you hate gay bars, especially l'Entr'acte."

"You're quite right. But Sarah and I were eating out on Prince-Arthur, so we made an exception," Judy replied, glancing toward the bar.

Harry followed her gaze. Sarah Reid, the woman who had replaced her in Judy's life, was standing beside Raven. She was trying to get Francine's attention. Sarah was shorter than Raven, and her fine, fly-away hair was longer than Harry remembered. It appeared that she had put on some weight since Harry had seen her last.

"And don't look so resentful, although I must say that it's just like you to take things personally."

"What are you talking about?" Harry turned back to look at Judy, who had an irritated expression on her face.

"You're not the centre of the universe, you know. I mean, I didn't show up just to annoy you," insisted Judy. "I didn't even know you were coming here tonight."

Why was Judy protesting so strongly? And why did her protestations sound so false? Or did they? Was Harry simply overreacting?

"I'm not taking things personally," Harry responded, her tone mild because she wanted to avoid getting into an argument with Judy.

"Of course you're not," Judy said sarcastically.

"Listen, I didn't appreciate being spoken to like that when we were together, and I certainly don't now," said Harry, her mild tone becoming a bit strident.

"Be a bitch, then. You never did want to hear anything unpleasant about yourself."

"A *bitch*? Are you talking about Harriet? You obviously don't know her very well, then," Raven interjected. She had come up behind Harry without either of the older women noticing.

Judy stared at Raven, frowning as she took in Raven's youth and her punk appearance.

"Here, honey," Raven added. She handed Harry a bottle of mineral water and then slid her arm around Harry's waist.

Honey? Since when? Raven detested teams of endearment. Harry stifled a grin. She calmed down and put her arm around Raven's shoulder. Judy looked shocked, which had obviously been Raven's intent.

"So who's this?" asked Raven. "Somebody you know?"

Raven's attitude was so in-your-face that Harry knew she must have overheard her conversation with Judy.

"This is Judy Johnson. Judy, this is my girlfriend, Raven Stone. From San Francisco."

"Oh, yes — I remember you mentioning something about her," Raven said with a dismissive nod.

Harry lost her nerve. "Want to dance?" she asked, attempting to get Raven away from Judy before her ex-lover recovered her equilibrium. But Raven was evidently enjoying herself too much to respond.

"*This* is who you're dating?" Judy sounded incredulous.

Harry drew herself up. "Yes."

"You ought to be ashamed of yourself!"

Harry lost her temper. "You've got no right to speak to me like that! In fact, you've got no right to say anything to me at all, so just butt out, will you?"

Manon sauntered up behind Harry and Raven. "Hold on, ladies," she interjected. "Let's not get carried away, here."

"I should have known you would take her side," Judy raged.

Manon held up her hands in a gesture of capitulation. "Hey, I just wanted to ask Raven to dance."

Raven glanced at Harry, who gave her a nearly imperceptible nod, even though being left alone with Judy was not a fate she relished. She watched Manon and Raven walk to the dance floor, trying to ignore Judy's smouldering glare.

"You haven't changed much," she said abruptly, moving toward the wall to let several women pass.

Judy followed her. "Do you think my life has been a bed of roses these past eight months?"

"I wouldn't know," Harry responded. She took a swig of water, hoping it would dissolve the lump in her throat.

"Being in a new relationship isn't easy," Judy said.

Did Judy regret having left her? Harry wondered. Did she care if Judy regretted leaving her? Harry gave her ex-lover a sharp look and then, for lack of an appropriate response, finished her bottle of water.

"You must feel the same way," added Judy.

Since there was no more water to drink, Harry busied herself searching for a place to deposit the empty bottle.

"Well, don't you?"

Harry placed the bottle on the counter running along the back of the bar and sat down on a stool. So much for diversionary tactics; Judy was obviously on a roll, and Harry was in her way.

"And she's so young."

"Stop it, Judy," Harry grumbled. "You were the one who walked out, so how can you stand there and pretend to be concerned about what I do or whom I get involved with?"

Judy's faced reddened. She was about to say something when her lover, Sarah Reid, approached them with a glass of wine in each hand, one white, the other red. She gave the glass of white wine to Judy and said, "Hello, Harry."

When Harry saw that Sarah was carefully refraining from looking directly at her, she acknowledged her with a rather curt nod, but that was all. Once upon a time, Sarah had been Harry's friend. But when Judy and Sarah became lovers, Harry realized that she didn't have to turn the other cheek when she was betrayed. Learning that it was all right to be angry had been a liberating feeling. It came back to her now as she stared at the tense expressions on their faces. Suddenly she felt disgusted with their posturing. They had been arguing with each other in the washroom, and their appearance of solidarity was obviously for her benefit only.

She pushed a rebellious lock of hair from her forehead, abruptly said, "Have a nice evening," and stalked off. It served them right to be alone with each other.

She half expected Judy to call out, but she didn't. Not that Harry was disappointed; she could only hang on to her illusions for so long, and eight months was a bit too protracted, even for someone as loyal as she was. She hadn't wanted her relationship with Judy to end, but, once it had, there was no going back. On an emotional level, she hadn't realized that until tonight.

Bloody hell.

She squeezed through the crowd, making her way to the back of the bar. Raven was still dancing with Manon, and Sue, Marg, Liz and Sophie were also on the dance floor. This time, Marg and Sophie were together. With Marg's curly black hair and Sophie's dark eyes, they made an interesting couple. She walked past them, her eyes tearing from the thick smoke.

The door leading to the back patio was ajar, and she impulsively pushed it open and walked outside. The cold bit into her flesh, making her shiver. She took a shallow breath of chilled air. Cold or not, the fresh air felt good in her lungs.

Snow was still falling, but not as heavily. The wind had subsided to a gentle breeze which playfully swirled the flakes. Harry stood close to the door, under the sloping roof which covered nearly half of the patio. During summer, when the patio was in use, the roof kept the rain off the tables closest to the building.

Harry could see the outline of stacked plastic tables and chairs through the winter's accumulation of snow. One stack of chairs seemed to have fallen over, perhaps unbalanced by a strong gust of wind.

Harry squinted in the dim light, moved a bit closer and changed her mind. The lump in the snow was too low to the ground, too smooth and too lacking in angles to be chairs. Perhaps it was a folded-up market umbrella.

Harry was drawn to the lump in the snow like a moth to light. She edged closer until she was standing over it. She fought against recognition of what the lump most certainly was, trying to convince herself otherwise. But it wasn't a furled market umbrella or a stack of chairs fallen on its side. A market umbrella wouldn't have been wearing the black high-heel shoe which had fallen off and was lying forlornly to one side. And a stack of chairs didn't possess a sheer black stocking which was slightly wet from the snow that had blown under the roof of the patio.

Harry fell to her knees, her heart thumping faster than the beat of the dance music coming from inside the bar. Then she slowly reached down and brushed the thin layer of snow from Julie Beliveau's lifeless face.

A beefy cop pulled the jukebox plug from the wall socket and the booming dance music abruptly halted. The lights came on, and police swarmed over the bar like bees suddenly chancing upon a field of clover. Dancers stopped in their tracks, women cut conversations short, lovers necking in dark corners instantly broke apart. The silence was unnatural. Many women stood up, uncertain expressions on their faces, their eyes red-rimmed from having spent a long evening in a smoky bar.

Harry glanced at her watch. It was nearly two-thirty in the morning.

In the old days, before the Stonewall Riots and the rise of the gay and lesbian liberation movements, police had often raided Montreal's gay and lesbian bars, arresting their patrons, tossing them in paddy-wagons, carting them off to police stations and locking them up until they could be hauled before a judge. Criminal charges were laid and lives were ruined. Even after the gay community organized, it wasn't unusual for Montreal Urban Community cops to conduct raids when the city fathers believed they had good reason to rid the city of some of its least desirable elements, or at least stop them from publicly socializing with each other for a while. This had happened around the time of the Montreal Olympics, and several years later, just before the Pope's visit to the city.

More recently, police would drop by unannounced, turn on the lights and count heads to ensure that the bars weren't filled over their posted limit, and check IDs to make sure no one was underage. Patrons saw such invasions as harassment, and as collaboration between the gay community and the police increased, raids and impromptu visits grew less frequent.

It had therefore been a long time since most of the women in l'Entr'acte had weathered a police invasion, especially the size of the one that took place not long after Harry rushed back into the bar, securely closing the patio door behind her. She searched out Raven and Manon, who were still dancing. With a few carefully chosen words, she informed Manon that her twin sister's lover was most certainly dead. The three of them rushed to the front of the bar, Manon to break the news to her sister, Harry and Raven to the pay phone in the vestibule. Harry dialled 911 and reported Julie's death.

And now the police had arrived. Harry soon lost track of how many there were. She squeezed Raven's hand and looked at the smoke-discoloured walls and the stained wood floor. L'Entr'acte was so shabby that she felt a momentary sense of shame that she and her friends patronized it without a second thought. Why didn't Montreal have a clean, spacious, well-ventilated lesbian bar? Once the last police officer rushed past, she and Raven went to the bar, where Manon was standing over Francine, who was slouched on a stool. There was a stunned expression on her face. A cup of coffee was sitting on the bar in front of her.

Harry reached out to touch Francine's shoulder. "I'm sorry."

Francine roughly brushed Harry's hand away. "For what? That you didn't get into her pants before she died?"

Harry recoiled in shock.

"Francine!" Manon chastised her sister. "That's not fair! She doesn't mean it, Harry; she's too upset to realize what she's saying."

Harry controlled herself. If Francine didn't want her sympathy, she wasn't going to get it. She moved away from them and leaned against the bar. Raven swiftly followed.

"I can't believe she said that to you," Raven said in a low voice.

"Neither can I," sighed Harry. "But she's always been tough, and I guess Julie's death isn't going to change that. Maybe it's the only way she can deal with it."

"Did Julie really sleep around?"

"There were rumours. She flirted with everyone at one time or another. This weekend, it just happened to be me, and Francine caught her at it."

A deep-voiced, plain-clothed police officer broke the protracted silence. "Where's Harriet Hubbley? The woman who found the body?" he asked in French.

"Here." Harry stood up.

"Would you mind coming with me?" he asked, switching to slightly accented English.

Raven reached out and touched her arm. "Do you want me to go with you?"

"No, I'll be fine."

"I'll wait here, then."

Harry nodded and followed the tall, husky police officer to the back of the bar. The patio door was now standing wide open. Snow was blowing into the bar, and the floor was streaked with dirty water. Women who had been seated in that area or who had been standing at the far end of the counter had been moved toward the front of the bar, and uniformed police officers were questioning them singly and in small groups.

He sat down at a table. "I'm Lieutenant-Detective Claude Gagnon," he said, thumbing through a rather grimy notebook until he came to a blank page. Then he pulled a pen from the inner pocket of his suit jacket. "Could you please spell your name for me? I'll also need your address and telephone number."

Harry sat at the chair across from him and gave him that information.

"It's a hell of a cold night," he continued. "Why did you go outside?"

Harry certainly wasn't going to tell him that she had been fed up with the complex interplay among herself, her ex-lover, her ex-lover's new lover and her current girlfriend, not to mention Julie, now lying dead in the snow, as well as Julie's lover, Francine; Francine's twin sister, Manon; and Manon's lover, Sue.

"It was hot in here, and smoky. I stepped out for a breath of fresh air."

"Right," he muttered in a disbelieving voice. "Why did you go out on the patio instead of out front, where everybody else was?"

"Because I was in the back of the bar at the time, and the door was ajar," Harry answered.

This elicited a glimmer of interest. "Was it, now? By how much?"

"Just a little."

"An inch or a foot?"

Harry thought back. "More than an inch, or I likely wouldn't have noticed it," she replied. "But not as much as a foot or snow would have been coming in, and I don't remember the floor being wet. But I'm sure the people who were seated at the tables near the door would be able to tell you whether it was or not. They must have felt a draft, although I doubt they would have bothered to close the door. As I said, it was hot and smoky."

The detective nodded. "When you were out on the patio, did you see anything except Madame Beliveau's body?"

"Like what?"

"Anything," he said rather impatiently.

His manners could certainly use some improving. "There were stacked patio tables and chairs. They were covered with a lot of snow."

"How do you know they were patio tables and chairs?" he asked suspiciously.

"Because I've been here during the summer when they've been in use."

"You didn't see any footprints in the snow?"

"I didn't notice. But I suppose there were. I walked around out there, and so did Julie."

"How well did you know the deceased?"

"We went to university together. And we've stayed in touch ever since."

"You mean that you were good friends?"

"Not really," Harry answered. She paused because she wasn't sure how to explain her relationship with Julie to Lieutenant-Detective Gagnon. He hadn't known Julie, which placed him at a distinct disadvantage when it came to understanding how Julie related to women. "I suppose you could say we were friends, but not close friends."

He closed his notebook and stared at Harry. He had such a disgusted expression on his face that she knew he didn't believe her. He looked around and frowned. "That's all for now. But don't leave town. I'll be getting back to you before long."

Don't leave *town*? "Was Julie Beliveau *murdered*?"

Gagnon momentarily raised his querulous eyes from the notes he was scribbling in what looked like an indecipherable script. He obviously wasn't used to people asking questions while he was interrogating them. Perhaps he had been roused from a sound sleep by the ringing of his telephone. Or maybe he was homophobic.

He stared at her long and hard. "*Mais oui, madame*. Of course. What did you think? Why else would the Homicide Squad be here? And why else would I be asking all these questions in the middle of the night instead of letting everyone go home to bed?"

"I didn't know," Harry said in a near-whisper.

"But you wiped the snow from her face. Didn't you see the blood on the side of her head and the brick lying beside her body?"

Harry thought back to when she had brushed the thin layer of snow from Julie's face and how cold her skin had been. Her stomach churned. "No, I didn't."

"You didn't notice very much, did you?"

What did he mean by that? Harry glanced at him. His intelligent eyes were studying her, but the shrewd expression on his face gave nothing away. She refrained from replying; there was nothing she could say, anyway. She had impulsively gone out on the patio, which hadn't been very well lit. She had been preoccupied with Raven's sudden reappearance in her life and with seeing Judy and Sarah for the first time in eight months. It had been dreadfully cold out, and once she had discovered Julie's body she hadn't stuck around very long.

"Maybe she was mugged," Harry said. "Perhaps someone wanted to rob her."

"We thought of that, but it doesn't seem as if anything was taken," Gagnon responded. "We found her purse under her body. Her wallet and a credit-card holder were in it, and it didn't look as if anything was missing. We'll check that more closely, of course. Now, is there anything else you would like to tell me?" he asked, leaning closer.

Harry could smell cigarette smoke on his breath, but she made an effort not to move back because she didn't want to antagonize him.

"No."

He pursed his lips. "Are you certain?"

"Very."

He stood up abruptly. "I'll be in touch, then."

That sounded more like a warning than a statement of fact, but Harry just nodded. She felt like she had been flattened by a steam-roller.

Lieutenant-Detective Gagnon pulled up the collar of his coat and went outside on the patio. Harry rose from the chair and returned to the front of the bar.

A large pot of coffee, a carton of milk, a bowl of sugar and several mismatched coffee mugs were sitting on the bar. Next to them was an uncorked bottle of cognac and several brandy snifters.

"What will you have? Coffee or cognac?" the lone woman behind the bar asked in French. Harry knew that her first name was Gabriella and that she often worked with Francine. Gabriella had two small children at home, both conceived through artificial insemination.

"Some of each," Harry replied in the same language. "But I'll fix it myself."

Gabriella nodded and leaned her elbows on the bar. "*D'accord*. No problem. You know, we've never had someone die here before."

"I suppose not," Harry replied. She filled a mug with coffee and then poured a small amount of cognac in it.

"What did she die of? A heart attack?"

If Gabriella didn't know that Julie had been murdered, then most likely Francine, Manon and the others weren't aware of it, either.

"I'm not sure," Harry prevaricated, thinking that it might be to her advantage to keep the truth concealed for the moment. Harry's investigative instincts had been roused, and the fact that it might not be fair to keep the news of Julie's murder secret never entered her mind.

Gabriella took a damp rag and wiped the bar. "I guess we'll find out soon enough."

Harry nodded. "I'm sure we will."

Two tables at the front of the bar had been commandeered by her friends. Manon was sitting with her arm around Francine's shoulder, and Sue Phillips, Marg Alexander and Sophie Lister formed a protective circle around them. Judy and Sarah were seated close together at the second table, while Raven was leaning against the wall, a mug of steaming coffee in her hand. She had retrieved her coat from the coat check and draped it over her shoulders. Harry walked over to her, slumped against the wall and put her arm around Raven. Cold seeped through the wall into her back, but she didn't move.

Harry studied her friends' faces, pallid under the bare lightbulbs hanging from the timbered, smoke-blackened ceiling. Was there a killer among them? She chided herself for being an idiot; of course there was. It wouldn't be the first time someone she knew had resorted to violence. Had Julie the flirt merely been a tease, or had she taken lovers? Just how possessive was Francine? Would she have killed her lover for being unfaithful?

Manon bent over and said something to Sue, who nodded and got up. She paused for a moment and then approached Harry. "I'm going to get the car so we can drive Francine home. Would you come with me? I don't feel like going alone."

"Of course," Harry said automatically. She turned to Raven as an afterthought. "You don't mind, do you?"

"No. Go on. I'll be fine," she assured Harry.

"I'll be back before long."

Harry and Sue handed the coat check woman their chits and retrieved their jackets.

"Where's your car?" asked Harry.

"In a parking lot a couple of blocks west of here."

Snow crunched underfoot as they walked up the steps to the sidewalk. It was after three in the morning and the city was as quiet as it ever got.

"I suppose Francine's pretty upset," Harry ventured.

Sue glanced at Harry. When she finally replied, her tone was bitter. "Why don't you just come right out and say it?"

Harry nearly asked "Say what?," but she shut her mouth and wrapped her scarf around her face before the words had a chance to form on her lips.

They turned off rue St-Denis and began walking toward the parking lot. The wind gathered strength and began to blow out of the northwest. Harry shoved her gloved hands in the pockets of her leather jacket and trudged on.

"You don't have to play innocent for my sake," Sue added.

"I'm not," responded Harry. But if anyone was innocent, it was her.

"For a long time, everybody knew what was going on between Manon and Julie except for Francine and me," Sue eventually said.

Harry's mouth dropped open behind her scarf. Perhaps "innocent" hadn't been the right word to describe her condition. But then, she had been rather preoccupied with relationship troubles of her own these past few years.

"I felt like such a fool when I discovered that they were lovers," Sue continued. "Here I thought Manon had finally matured enough to settle down, but that wasn't it at all. She was so busy with Julie that she didn't have time for other women. Francine and I were the perfect foils, weren't we? The four of us had been friends for years, and everyone was used to the way Julie flirted with Manon and the way Manon teased her back. They got away with murder right in front of our eyes, but neither of us suspected a thing. Here's the parking lot." Sue abruptly veered left, leaving Harry to stumble after her.

As soon as Sue unlocked the passenger-side door, Harry slid in. The interior of the car was icy. Sue turned the key in the ignition and the car started on the first try. Then she flicked the fan on high. "It should warm up in a minute or two."

Harry gathered her wits about her. "When did you find out?"

"Julie's dead now," Sue said, her tone unemotional. She removed her cap and her auburn hair fell to her shoulders. "So does it really matter?"

Very much so, Harry reflected.

"Listen, why is it taking so long for the police to release Julie's body? Francine wants to call a funeral home and have them pick it up before she leaves the bar."

It was now or never, Harry decided. If she delayed telling the truth any longer, her relationship with her friends would likely be damaged.

"Because Julie was murdered."

It was late. Harry was so tired that her senses were preternaturally alert. She was seated on the leather sofa in Francine and Julie's living room. Marg Alexander was sitting beside her, and Sophie Lister was on the other sofa. Nobody was talking; whether this was because of exhaustion or because they didn't have anything to say, Harry didn't know. Judy, Sarah and Liz Martin were in the dining room, sitting at one end of the large wood table, talking quietly among themselves. Judy had always liked Liz, possibly because she was so malleable. The more Harry thought about it, the less she understood why she had been so much in love with Judy. Maybe Judy had changed. On the other hand, maybe Harry had changed. Harry was too fatigued to think it through.

As soon as they had arrived at the boulevard St-Joseph flat, Manon had fed Francine a sleeping pill and bustled her off to bed. Raven had busied herself in the kitchen, making a pot of strong coffee and boiling water for tea. She had rummaged through the fridge and prepared sandwiches, which she served with celery and carrot sticks and glasses of orange juice. She had forced them to eat whether they were hungry or not, and everyone revived, at least for a time. But no one went home. Perhaps, like Harry, they took some small comfort in being with one another.

Manon came into the living room and sprawled beside Sophie. "Francine's fallen asleep."

"That's good," Harry remarked. "Perhaps we should leave now and let her get some rest."

Manon ignored her, as did Sue when she entered the room a few minutes later. Sophie moved over, and Sue sat close beside Manon, putting her hand on her lover's knee.

So that was how it was going to be, Harry thought, too weary to feel resentful. Solidarity despite Manon's treacherous betrayal. Sue had stopped talking to Harry as soon as she dropped the bombshell about Julie having been murdered. There had been an immediate rift between them, and Sue had driven to l'Entr'acte without uttering another word. She had parked illegally outside the bar and rushed inside, presumably to tell the others the truth about how Julie had died.

When it became apparent that they were going to snub her, Harry got up and left the living room. Perhaps she should have shown more loyalty to her friends by immediately telling them that Julie had been killed by person or persons still unknown. But she had investigated so many unnatural deaths in the past few years that her instincts had automatically kicked in when she learned Julie had been murdered. In hindsight, she realized that it had been wrong not to tell her friends the truth as soon as Lieutenant-Detective Gagnon finished questioning her. She had managed to extract one piece of vital information from Sue, but in the process she had alienated both Sue and Manon, and perhaps some of the others. It was becoming increasingly clear that an apology was in order.

The conversation abruptly stopped when Harry entered the dining room.

"I see you're up to your usual tricks again." Judy's tone was curt, her expression irritatingly gratified.

"What are you talking about?"

"Don't try to fool me."

"How would you know if I was?"

Judy gave a short, scornful laugh. "I only lived with you for twelve years."

Why had Harry never noticed how vexatious Judy could be? She was beginning to question her taste in women. "You weren't very perceptive then either."

"Don't give me that," Judy said scornfully. "You've always been an emotional coward, and the fact that you've taken up with that teenage punk only proves my point."

It finally dawned on her: Judy was jealous! Harry started to laugh, which made Judy all the more furious.

"How dare you —"

"Oh, be quiet," Harry sputtered. "I wish I had realized what you were like years ago," she added. While she was being candid, she might as well go all the way. She did an about-face, returned to the living room and perched on the edge of the coffee table in front of Manon and Sue.

Manon looked startled, but Sue continued to ignore her.

"Listen, I apologize for not telling you what happened to Julie as soon as I found out," Harry said. "It was stupid of me not to. I hope you'll overlook my lapse in judgment."

Sue's eyes snapped to attention, but she didn't say anything. Manon looked too drained to respond.

"Anyway, we can talk about it later," Harry said swiftly. She got up and left. Perhaps once they thought about what she had said, they would realize that there was no point in holding a grudge. This time Judy, Sarah and Liz were silent when she passed through the dining room, although they stared at her so intently that Harry felt like their eyes were burning a hole in her back. She hurried past the bedroom and went into the kitchen. At this rate she would have to decamp to the balcony to escape from one hostile camp or another.

Raven was sitting in one of the kitchen chairs, her head and arms resting on the table. She was sound asleep, her breathing slow and regular. There was an empty coffee cup, a half-consumed sandwich and several celery sticks on a plate in front of her. Harry sat down. She picked up one of the celery sticks and bit it in half, intent on chewing silently. She soon learned that quietly crunching on celery was an impossibility.

"Harry?"

"Sorry. I didn't mean to wake you up."

Raven raised her head and gave Harry a sleepy grin. "You sound like a garbage compactor."

Since she had never heard a garbage compactor at work, Harry wasn't about to argue. "Anything to turn you on, my love," she said lightly. "Are you ready to go home?"

Raven glanced at her watch. It was a modern contraption with barely recognizable numbers and no discernible hands, but she seemed to have no difficulty reading it.

"I guess so. What's going to happen tomorrow? Will the rest of your convention be cancelled?"

"That's a good question," said Harry.

Manon walked into the kitchen, poured herself a cup of coffee and leaned against the counter. She looked like hell frozen over. Her usually cheerful expression had disappeared, and Harry could see the woman she would be ten or fifteen years from now.

"*Bon*," Manon said tiredly.

"I think that means she wants to talk to you," Raven surmised. Before Harry could dispute her interpretation of Manon's intentions, Raven got up and left the room.

Manon reached out and closed the door. "She's pretty smart for someone so young."

"She's twenty-five."

"That's what I said."

Harry knew when she was licked. "I hear you. But she's mature for her age."

"You should know," Manon said. She sounded preoccupied. "Listen, we have to talk, you and I."

"About the brunch at your house, you mean."

Manon carried her cup to the table and sat down in the chair Raven had vacated. "There's nothing to discuss about that. Even if we wanted to cancel, there's no way to reach everyone in time. We invited a lot of people — not only our close friends, but also acquaintances and people from out of town. They're going to show up at my place tomorrow morning, so it has to go on, despite Julie's death."

"That's going to be difficult for you," Harry commented.

Manon shrugged. "I'll manage. I *have* to manage. You could help by coming early and sticking around for the duration — that way I can disappear if I want to."

Harry could do that. It would be penance of a sort, which fit her current state of mind perfectly. "Fine."

"But that's not what I wanted to talk to you about," Manon said. "I know that you meant what you said back there in the living room. Sue's still mad, but she'll cool off eventually. You and I go back too far for me to stay pissed off for long. Besides, everybody's got the right to do something stupid once in a while."

Harry didn't reply. She deserved to be put in her place, but, even so, she hated eating crow.

"I hear that you managed to worm everything out of Sue," Manon added abruptly.

Harry wouldn't have described her conversation with Sue that way, but she kept quiet. She picked up a celery stick and chewed on it.

"I never meant to get involved with Julie," Manon insisted. "We didn't run into each other after we graduated, but when she started going out with Francine, Sue and I started to see Julie on a regular basis. Francine and I have always been close. We probably understand each other better than most people, despite the fact that I went to university and she dropped out before she finished high school."

"I can see that," Harry agreed. She got up, poured herself a cup of coffee and sat down at the table again.

"It's no secret that Sue and I have had our problems over the years. I dearly love her, but somehow I've never been able to settle down. Of course Sue deserves better."

Harry gathered it was now her opportunity to comment, but she refrained.

"Since when have you become a diplomat?" asked Manon.

"I don't know what you're talking about."

"Tell me another one. Anyway, it doesn't matter; I know what you think. Actually, it's what, *everybody* thinks, but I can't help that. To quote Popeye, 'I yam what I yam.'"

Harry stifled a grin.

"Julie came on to anyone who had a pulse," Manon said crudely. "Man, she was *dangerous* in the old days. You know what I mean — viby as hell. Most women couldn't take it — they walked before things got serious. Still, she had quite a few lovers over the years. Nobody ever stuck with her for long. She was way too hot. Then I made the mistake of introducing her to Francine, who took one look at her and fell for her like a ton of bricks. It seemed to be mutual, but I knew better. There was no way in the world that I would ever have trusted Julie not to fuck Francine over. When they first got together, I told Francine she was being stupid, that Julie was going to cheat on her. But Francine was macho enough to think that she could scratch Julie's itch."

That particular image was a bit too graphic for Harry. She finished her coffee and then fidgeted with her mug.

"The trouble with you is that you've never been able to deal with sexual stuff. Listen, it's not dirty, it's *life*. Julie was primal. She had *needs*. Francine tried, but she wasn't able to fulfil them."

"Hmm," Harry remarked.

"Julie did care deeply about Francine, though. She settled down, maybe because being with Francine was different. See, Francine really loved her, and I don't think that had ever happened to Julie before. Women would go into a frenzy over Julie, but it was generally sexual. She made women want her, but most of the time that was as far as it went. But Francine was just plain crazy about her. Julie was sexy and she liked to flaunt it and to flirt, but after she and Francine got together she didn't get involved with women who came on to her."

"Until you."

"Until me," Manon nodded glumly.

"How long were the two of you lovers?" Harry asked.

Manon made a face. She obviously felt guilty, and Harry could understand why; she had betrayed her twin sister.

"You know how it is," Manon said with a self-deprecating shrug. "It all started innocently enough, with a double date one New Year's. Julie got drunk, and she was all over everybody: Francine, Sue, me and several other women who were there. That was okay, everybody sort of expected it. There's always at least one woman who gets soused out of her mind at every New Year's party and lives to regret it the next morning. But then Julie corralled me in the bathroom just after midnight and started touching me. Well, I had had a little too much to drink myself, and, before I knew it, things got steamy. I pushed her away before it got out of hand, but what happened stayed in my mind. That's not something you forget overnight."

"I suppose not."

"I started feeling restless, and one night, when Sue was out for the evening and I knew Francine was working, I called their place. I told myself that I just wanted to talk to her, but down deep I knew better. She invited me over, and we ended up in bed together. I suppose I knew we would, but I wasn't admitting it to myself."

Imagine bedding your sister's lover in her own home. What if Francine had left work early that night?

"When was that?"

"A little over two years ago."

"And Francine didn't know?"

"Of course not," Manon said indignantly. "We were careful."

"But Sue discovered what you were up to," Harry remarked.

Manon made a face. "Eventually. She knows me too well. When I stopped cruising, she got suspicious. She figured I had someone steady on the side, but for the longest time she didn't know who it was."

"How did she find out?"

"I told her."

That drew Harry's attention. "You did?"

"Do you think Sue and I never talked about what was really going on?" Manon asked impatiently. "We wouldn't have lasted all these years if I hadn't been honest."

Harry looked sceptical.

"Well, mostly honest," Manon conceded. "I didn't always tell Sue about the women I was seeing. Sometimes I wondered whether I should mention anything at all because it was so painful for her. But it was pointless to lie; there are too many gossips in the lesbian community. Montreal's a big city, but somebody always finds out in the end."

That much was true, Harry thought. "When did you tell Sue about Julie?"

"What difference does that make?"

A hell of a lot, depending on what "not long ago" meant. What if it had been a couple of days before Julie was killed? Or a few hours before someone launched a brick at Julie's head? Discovering that Manon and Julie were lovers would have given Sue an incredibly strong motive to want Julie out of the way.

"Frankly, I was terrified when Julie and I became lovers," Manon admitted. She folded her hands on the table, looked down at them and then swiftly unfolded them and slid them under the table. "I couldn't imagine what would happen if Francine found out."

"I'll bet."

"But Julie got under my skin. And once she got her claws into me, she didn't want to let go. Don't look at me like that. You've always been the sane one about sex, at least until recently. Listen, what are you doing with someone like Raven, anyway?"

"Don't try to change the subject."

"You know me too well," Manon said. "God, I wish I still smoked."

To Harry, smoking was related to being young and sexually confused, and to long, sleepless nights. She could therefore understand why Manon was tempted.

"Maybe there's some wine," Manon commented. She got up and opened the fridge.

"You don't need anything to drink," said Harry. She glanced at her watch; it was nearly five o'clock in the morning. "We're going to feel like hell tomorrow as it is."

Manon closed the fridge and turned to face Harry. "You're right. But I wish you wouldn't be so hard on me. I could feel your disapproval all the way from the living room. I'm only human, after all."

"I know," Harry said. But to have an affair with your twin sister's lover! Manon's audacity took Harry's breath away, and that was without considering the ethics of the situation. "Julie was with you tonight, wasn't she?"

Manon nodded. "Yes. I'm sorry that Francine blamed you for it, but I obviously couldn't say anything to let you off the hook. She came with me when I went to move the car. After we fooled around a little, we split up and arrived at l'Entr'acte separately."

That cleared up one mystery, but there were still a few hundred others to be resolved.

"You know, there's one word I haven't heard you mention," Harry remarked.

"And what's that?"

"Love," Harry said in a soft voice.

Manon looked taken aback. She was about to reply when the kitchen door opened and Isabelle hurried into the room.

"*C'est vrai?* Is it true?" she asked, her voice shrill. "Julie is dead? *Murdered?*"

Manon swiftly rose from her chair and gave her younger sister a hug. "It's true, Isabelle. Come, sit down."

Isabelle dithered until her husband, Albert, strode into the kitchen.

"How did it happen?" she asked.

"Who did it?" demanded Albert.

"The police may have some ideas, but they haven't chosen to impart them to us," Harry remarked. She stood up and, seconds later, Isabelle collapsed into the chair she vacated.

"What are you talking about?" Albert asked, his voice shrill.

"You don't think that one of us murdered Julie!" Isabelle asked.

"She didn't say that, Isabelle," Manon interrupted somewhat impatiently.

"No, but that's what she means," Isabelle insisted.

The three of them turned and stared at Harry, who felt like a deer caught in the headlights of an oncoming car.

"I do not," she sputtered. Which was a lie, because of course she did. Who else had killed Julie Beliveau if not someone she knew? It was unlikely that Julie had been murdered by a stranger, after all.

"Well!" Isabelle huffed. "Just because we happened to spend a good part of the evening in a bistro on rue St-Denis doesn't mean we had anything to do with Julie's death."

"We were with friends all evening, and we can prove it," Albert asserted, reverting to formal French.

Someone had a guilty conscience, Harry reflected, her attention piqued. But about what?

"Why would you need to?" she responded in the same language.

Albert and Isabelle sputtered and denied everything up to and including original sin. While Harry was somewhat amused by their filibuster, she was also depressed; Julie had been part of their entourage as Francine's partner for five years, and yet all Isabelle and Albert were interested in was proving that they had nothing to do with her death. She could understand Albert not really caring, because it was evident that he had never been that fond of his sisters-in-law, much less their partners. But Isabelle's attitude was another matter. She thought about telling them to shut up, but didn't. Instead, she waited for them to wind down.

"You might want to tell that to the police," Harry announced, not waiting for what she assumed would be yet another explosive reaction. She left the kitchen and went into the dining room, relieved to find it empty. Given her ex-lover's attitude, Harry would be no further ahead if she traded Isabelle and Albert for Judy and Sarah. Perhaps Judy and Sarah had gone home. Actually, that sounded like a good idea. Harry had likely discovered all there was to learn for one evening, so there was no point in staying any longer. All she had to do was find Raven, then she could go home herself.

In the corner of the dining room was a bay window which overlooked the back lane. Two high-backed wing chairs sat in the tiny alcove. Harry walked over to the window. Frost coated the bottom of the windowpane. She pressed her nose against the cold glass and looked out into the backyard.

"I didn't kill her."

Harry was so startled that she banged her forehead against the window.

"Francine?"

"*Oui.*"

"I thought you were asleep."

"You and everybody else," Francine said softly. "But it takes more than a sleeping pill to put me out for long. Why don't you join me?"

Had Francine been awake all evening? "How long have you been here?"

"I woke up just a few minutes ago. It's nearly morning, isn't it?"

"Yes." Harry turned around and looked at Francine, but the dining-room chandelier had been turned down low and she couldn't see her face. That put her at a disadvantage, but she was tired unto exhaustion, so she sat in the empty chair and stared out of the window. Her thoughts were disorganized, but she no longer cared. The wing chair was padded in just the right places. Her mind drifted and she did nothing to stop it, even though she knew she should try to think rationally. Once family and friends rallied round to support Francine, Harry might not get another opportunity to question her alone.

"Has someone accused you of murder?" Harry eventually asked.

Francine gave a low-throated chuckle. "Don't try to be cute, Hubbley. You know as well as I do that the lover is always the first person to be suspected. Am I right?"

Had Francine surmised that Julie was involved with someone else? Had she known it was Manon? Would Francine have been angry enough to kill her unfaithful lover?

"Let me put it another way, then. Am I wrong?"

"How would I know? I don't work for the police," Harry bluffed. Francine had always been shrewd, so Harry fully expected to get creamed for lying so blatantly. But Francine had other things on her mind.

"She was such a gorgeous woman. She was so good-looking and so sexy that I could hardly stand it," Francine said. Her voice was low, barely audible. "Goddammit, I *loved* her. And she loved me."

"It's hard," Harry commiserated.

"What the hell am I going to do without her?"

"It takes time —"

"Don't give me that shit." Francine's tone was scornful.

All right, so she had been about to unleash a platitude, but what did Francine want her to say? That she was going to suffer before things got better? Raven slid into the alcove, sparing Harry the necessity of responding.

"Everybody's gone except Manon and Sue, and I think they're planning to stay for a while," Raven said.

Harry stood up. She had had enough of the Lachance sisters for one night. "Let's go home, then."

Raven nodded.

"I'm sorry, about Julie," Harry said, in parting, to Francine.

There was no answer. Not that Harry had expected one.

Harry couldn't remember when she had been so tired. She barely had the energy to trudge through the snow.

"It's beautiful, isn't it?" Raven commented, her voice muffled by her scarf.

Harry raised her eyes from the sidewalk. The deserted, snow-covered expanse of Fletcher's Field lay before them.

"I love it," Raven said.

Much to Harry's amazement, Raven threw herself into a snowbank at the edge of the park.

"What are you *doing?*"

"Jeez, this stuff is cold!"

Harry started to laugh. Raven was covered with snow from head to foot. There was a clump of snow on her nose, and she looked incredibly silly. Harry's heart warmed.

"Join me," Raven said.

"Not on your life!"

"Come on, don't be such an old fogy!"

Old fogy? OLD FOGY? Was it the "old" or the "fogy" that sent Harry head first into the snowbank? She didn't know, and she didn't really care. She pulled her chin to her chest, did a somersault, and came up sputtering. Then she grinned and flopped on her back. The snow felt as soft as a bed of feathers. She looked up. The sky was filled with snowflakes, some of which fell on her face. They felt cold, like wet kisses. Raven was right; it *was* magical. She hadn't cavorted in the snow for longer than she could remember. She could recall having been frolicsome at one point in her life, but Judy had never indulged in horseplay.

"They don't taste like anything much," Raven commented.

Harry closed her eyes and opened her mouth, hoping that the pollution had long since been brought to earth by the snow that had already fallen.

"I love you, Harriet," Raven whispered.

Harry smiled and opened her eyes. Raven was already there, waiting for her. Raven's cheeks were cold and her eyebrows were coated with snow. Harry kissed her rather cautiously, worried that their lips would freeze together or that a cop would come along and rouse them from their icy love nest. The purity of the moment captivated her imagination in a way few things had in recent years.

"This is so cool," Raven remarked as they pulled apart.

"Isn't it, though?" Harry said with a smile. "We'd better be going."

Dawn was breaking as they mounted the steps to Harry's flat.

"I'm going to make love to you until you can't move," Raven threatened.

Harry fumbled in her pants pocket for her keys. "I'm so wiped that I can barely move now, so it's no contest."

"Don't give me that," scoffed Raven.

They tumbled into the house. After their walk from Francine's condo on boulevard St-Joseph and their sojourn in the snow, Harry's apartment felt overheated. She was sweating by the time she doffed her jacket and the rest of her winter duds.

"Come *on*," Raven coaxed.

Harry looked at Raven, who had already stripped to her undies, although that wasn't quite the right word for what she was wearing. Where did she get those incredible bras? Were there stores where only punks shopped?

Raven led Harry to the bedroom.

"I've been waiting for this all evening," Raven murmured as they fell to the bed. She took the lead and began removing Harry's clothes.

"Raven, I'm just too tired," Harry protested when Raven eased her over on her back and mounted her.

Raven looked questioningly at her, as if she was verifying the truth of her statement, and then withdrew. "I should be more sensitive to your needs."

"It's okay."

"No, it isn't," Raven insisted. "Look, I don't know these people, but they're old friends of yours. And one of them just got murdered. I should have realized you'd be too upset to make love."

Raven turned on her side and Harry cuddled against her back, uncertain about which part of Raven's declaration troubled her the most. Did Raven never get tired? Was that something that happened only in middle age? When had she lost the ability to stay up all night and still feel horny? On the other hand, she had had a long day, and someone she knew had been killed. Why shouldn't she be too beat to make love?

Still, Raven had flown in from San Francisco that same day, and she had been up all night, too. Ah, well. What difference did it make, anyway? She was twice Raven's age, although sometimes she would trade the meagre amount of wisdom she had gained in those extra twenty-five years for a little more stamina, especially between the sheets. Oh, vanity.

Raven soon dozed off, but Harry couldn't sleep. Once again, she was embroiled in a violent crime. Julie Beliveau was dead, murdered, her life snuffed out by someone wielding a brick. Everyone who had reason to want her dead had been in l'Entr'acte or in the vicinity when she had been killed.

Raven stirred, mumbled something indecipherable and tossed off the comforter. Harry glanced at her clock radio and sighed. It was nearly eight-thirty, and any possibility of sleep had fled with the night. She had to be at Manon and Sue's by eleven, and if she fell asleep now, she would never wake up, even if she set her alarm.

She carefully disengaged herself from Raven's grasp and slid out of bed. She retrieved her terrycloth robe from the bathroom, padded barefoot to the kitchen, took a can of coffee from the freezer and spooned enough for several cups into her percolator. Her stomach was both hungry and upset, likely because she had been awake throughout the night. While the coffee perked, she opened her fridge and peered inside. The view was depressing. There wasn't much to eat. A carton of skim-milk yoghurt, some hairy carrots, an orange. She pulled out a croissant, a tub of margarine and the orange. She closely inspected the croissant, which was several days old. When she couldn't find even a hint of mould on its surface, she decided that it was still edible. She wrapped the croissant in a paper towel and placed it on the rack in the microwave. While she waited for it to warm up, she remembered the fridge in Raven's apartment in San Francisco. Although Raven never seemed to shop, her fridge had always been packed with goodies: fruit juices; salad mixings; half-loaves of several varieties of bread, all of which seemed fresh; piquant spreads; and tangy dressings. Harry suddenly felt nostalgic for good food.

The microwave beeped. Harry removed the croissant, broke it apart and dabbed margarine on each section. Then she rapidly devoured it, licking her fingers when she was done. She had been hungrier than she realized.

Eenie-meenie-minie-mo, who had killed Julie-o? She ripped the peel from the orange and carefully separated the sections. She slipped them one by one between her lips and popped them with her teeth. There was something sensual about biting into the soft fruit and releasing its tart juice into her mouth.

Harry munched on orange pulp and made a mental list of suspects. Francine had been quite astute about her own potential culpability, and she had to be high on anybody's list. She had been Julie's partner and she was by nature a jealous woman. Still, she and Julie had been together for five years, and Francine swore that she loved her. Manon claimed that Julie had been faithful to Francine until Julie and Manon became lovers, but Manon might not be in possession of all the facts. Perhaps Julie had lied to Manon to build up Manon's ego. It was certainly something Julie had been capable of doing.

Even if Julie had regularly cheated on Francine, none of Julie's other lovers had suffered an untimely or suspicious death. Perhaps Francine had looked the other way because she was crazy about Julie. People made allowances for those they loved, and they often came to rather peculiar accommodations in their relationships. But what if Francine had discovered that Manon was Julie's lover? How forgiving would she have been about such a fundamental betrayal? The question was, had Francine known? Under the circumstances, she wasn't likely to say.

There was another possibility, of course — the fact that Francine, as co-owner of the boulevard St-Joseph property, would inherit it now that Julie was dead. The opportunity to gain possession of a property worth nearly half a million dollars might have provided a strong motive for murder, especially for someone who had never finished high school, who had worked all her life as a bartender and who had lived in a tiny flat in the east end before Julie had invited her to move in.

Manon Lachance could also be the guilty party. She and Julie had carried on a secret affair for two years, but how comfortable could their relationship have been? Manon had betrayed her twin sister, and Julie had betrayed her lover. Manon must have felt guilty, and yet her relationship with Julie hadn't been just a one-night stand. That, Harry could have understood, given both Julie's and Manon's passionate natures. But their affair had lasted, although it must have seared Manon's soul with shame. Still, that hadn't been enough to make her stop. And Julie — had her conscience been touched with guilt or hadn't she cared about the potential harm she was doing to her relationship with Francine?

What if Julie had threatened to tell Francine about their affair? Was she capable of blackmail? But following through on her threat would have exposed Julie's infidelity, too. What other reason would Julie have for blackmailing Manon? It wasn't as if Manon had a lot of money or assets other than the house in Montreal West, which she and Sue co-owned. Did Manon have other secrets that Julie had found out about?

Perhaps Manon had decided to stop seeing Julie, who then made a scene. Knowing Manon, she wouldn't have taken kindly to threats. Conversely, maybe Julie had decided to break it off, and Manon hadn't wanted their relationship to end. Harry could build scenario upon scenario until they tumbled down around her head, but she simply didn't know enough yet to say which, if any, was the right one.

And then there was Sue Phillips. She, too could have been the killer. For one thing, she had refused to tell Harry how long she had known about Manon and Julie's affair. And although that certainly hadn't been Manon's first liaison with another woman, it must have been abundantly clear to everyone who knew about it that it was different. Julie was *family*, both literally and figuratively, and it would have been impossible for Sue to suddenly avoid seeing Julie or Francine without arousing suspicion. Harry tried to imagine what it would be like to be constantly reminded of her lover's perfidy, and couldn't.

There were other suspects, as well. Harry thought back to the Friday-evening reception at the McGill Athletics Building when Marg Alexander had been noticeably agitated about what Julie had said to her. Had something been going on between Julie and Marg or had Julie simply been taunting her? And what about Isabelle Lachance and Albert Dack? Why had they been so fervent about protesting their innocence? But what motive did either of them have for wanting Julie dead?

And then there was Liz Martin, Harry mused, recalling how mesmer-ized Liz had looked after her close dance with Julie. Julie had been an annoying person, but was that enough to make someone attack her? If so, then nearly everyone who had known her had reason to kill her.

The fact that Julie had been hit with a brick suggested an impulsive rather than a premeditated attack. Julie had been strong, in good physical condition, so the attack must have been sudden, before Julie could react. Either she had known her assailant or someone had sneaked up behind her. But what was Julie doing out on the patio in the first place? Julie liked being in the thick of things, so she wouldn't have left the bar without a good reason. Had someone arranged to meet her secretly? Or had she, like Harry, seen that the door was ajar, looked outside, seen something strange and gone to investigate?

The killer had taken quite a risk, what with a packed bar just a few feet away. It was true that the door to the patio was always kept closed, and, in winter, the window was generally covered with frost, but still. Anyone could have acted precisely as Harry had and poked her head out for a breath of fresh air. Could have, but didn't, Harry reflected. At least not until the murderer had slipped back inside the bar or had made his or her getaway through the gate at the far end of the patio, which led to the lane. Another idea occurred to her. If Julie had secretly arranged to meet someone on the patio, her assailant might not have been in the bar at all that night. Like Isabelle Lachance and Albert Dack, for example.

Harry got up and poured herself another coffee.

Raven walked into the kitchen, rubbing the palm of her hand over her short hair. "Sure beats having to comb it," she remarked. She was wrapped in the comforter from the bed.

"I thought you were still asleep."

"The smell of good coffee wakes me every time," Raven replied. She reached out and stroked Harry's cheek. Then she kissed her.

It lasted for quite a while. Harry finally pulled away. "I thought you wanted some coffee."

"Coffee later, you now." Raven dropped the comforter. She was naked underneath. She pulled on one end of the belt of Harry's terrycloth robe.

Harry gently removed Raven's hands from her breasts. "I haven't got time, Raven. I have to be at Manon and Sue's before eleven."

Raven slumped against her. "Damn convention."

"I told you that I was busy," Harry reminded her. "Have some coffee. Then we'll shower and get dressed."

Raven retrieved the comforter from the floor, wrapped it tightly around her and poured herself a mug of coffee. She carried it to the table, added milk and sugar and sat down.

"I've never been in a place where the air was so cold," she said with a shiver.

"Do you want me to turn up the heat?"

"No. I don't think it would make any difference. Anyway, I'll get used to it eventually."

Harry topped up her coffee and sat in the chair opposite Raven.

"You know, I've been thinking about who killed Julie, and I know who murdered her," Raven said.

"But you don't even know any of the people involved."

"Neither do the police, and they solve crimes. Maybe not all of them, but some."

She had a point.

"Sometimes it's easier when you're a stranger and you can observe people from a distance," Raven remarked.

"So who do you think did it?"

"Your ex-lover, of course. What's her name again?"

Harry nearly dropped her mug. "WHAT?"

"Be careful — you almost spilled your coffee."

"Why on earth would you come to the conclusion that *Judy* killed Julie?"

"When we were at the bar last night, I saw Judy and Julie talking together," replied Raven.

"There was nothing unusual about that. They knew each other, after all," Harry pointed out.

"Yes, but you didn't see the expression on Judy's face. She looked both desperately in love and really angry," Raven explained.

Harry put her empty mug on the table and sat back. Really angry she could understand, but Judy desperately in love?

"Are you sure you've got the right person?"

"The woman you were arguing with when I came along with our drinks and wrapped myself around you?"

Harry grinned at the memory. "Yes."

"It was her, all right," confirmed Raven. "I was just passing by and it was noisy, so I couldn't hear what they were saying. But they were talking quite seriously. And Judy had that look on her face."

"What look?"

"You know, like she really wanted Julie."

Harry was incredulous, mainly because she hadn't seen *that* particular expression on Judy's face in more years than she cared to remember.

"I know what I'm talking about, Harriet," Raven insisted. "She was mad as hell, but she had this needy look on her face at the same time. She was leaning toward Julie, just *longing* for Julie to make her day."

Make her DAY?

"I assume it had something to do with sex," Raven said slyly. "Doesn't it always?"

Damn. She was right. Harry felt a mild twinge of jealousy, even though she no longer cared for Judy.

"You're not still in *love* with that woman, are you?"

If there was one thing which was vividly clear to Harry, that was it. She shook her head. "No. Definitely not."

"That's a relief," Raven said. "I would rather get involved with a scorpion than that bitch."

Raven wasn't exactly in a position to be the most rational judge of Judy's character, but Harry had to hand it to her. She wasn't all that far off.

"I still don't think that there was anything going on between Judy and Julie."

"Face it, love, you're not in a position to know," Raven said gently.

Raven was right. Judy could have been involved with any number of women, and unless she had come right out and told her, Harry never would have been any the wiser. But she couldn't help it if she took people at face value, believed what women told her and trusted her friends and lovers unless they proved themselves to be dishonest. If she hadn't outgrown her gullible tendencies by now, then she never would.

"Sorry. I didn't mean to disillusion you."

Harry got up and put her empty mug in the sink. "If that's what you saw, then that's what you saw."

"Are you mad at me?"

Harry turned around and leaned against the counter. Raven was slouched over the table, her chin in her hands. She looked as tired as Harry felt. "No. How could I be angry with you? You're just telling me what happened."

"But you sound so down."

"I'm tired, Raven. I didn't sleep at all last night, and I didn't get to bed until really late the night before that. I'm not overly fond of conventions, but this might be the last time I get to see some of these people. And I've been preoccupied with packing. I hadn't seen Judy or Sarah since Judy and I broke up, and she wasn't exactly friendly. And then Julie got killed."

"It's all been too much," said Raven.

"Well, yes," Harry said, realizing that it *had* been too much. She considered indulging in a good bout of self-pity, but resisted. She had quite enough on her plate at the moment.

Raven carried her cup to the sink, rinsed it and set it on a stack of plates. "And now you're trying to figure out who killed Julie, aren't you?"

Harry glanced at her. "How did you know?"

"You're forgetting that I was there when you were doing your sleuthing number in San Francisco," Raven reminded her. "And you did tell me about your trials and tribulations as an accidental detective in Provincetown and Nova Scotia."

"Not to mention Key West." Harry sighed.

Raven kissed her. "You don't *have* to, you know. You could just let the police do their job."

"I could, couldn't I?" Harry mused. It sounded so tempting. But even as she kissed Raven back, she knew it wasn't a real option. She took personally the murder of someone she knew. And her mind started working overtime when there was a homicide in her general vicinity.

"But you won't, will you?"

"No," Harry admitted.

"I didn't think so."

"Listen, we had better get dressed," Harry said. "I don't want to be late."

News of Julie's murder spread swiftly. But while those who knew her felt subdued, hardly anyone stayed away from the Sunday morning brunch scheduled at Manon and Sue's three-bedroom semi-detached house in Montreal West. Harry stood near the front door, greeting early arrivals and directing them to the ground-floor guest bedroom-cum-study, where coats and other winter gear were piled atop two single beds. At first she thought that people were a bit unfeeling; then she realized that no one had been aware of Manon and Julie's affair. Not many of them had been close to Julie, who had always been perceived as flighty. And since Francine wasn't a physical-education teacher, only Julie's closest friends knew her.

The houses in this Montreal West neighbourhood were certainly a long way from their student-day digs. When in university, many of them, including Harry, rented one- or two-bedroom flats in the blocks of apartment buildings and rooming houses in the area surrounding McGill University, which was known as the McGill Ghetto. Unlike today, when there are far too many graduates in every field of education, and many new teachers are unable to find work, jobs had been plentiful when Harry finished her degree. As soon as they were hired to teach for one of the local school boards, the vast majority of each successive graduating class put down payments on houses in West End — and traditionally English — neighbourhoods, including Montreal West, Notre-Dame-de-Grâce, Lower Westmount and parts of the West Island. But as long as Harry had been alone or involved in short-term relationships, she didn't even consider buying a house. She rented in downtown Montreal instead.

Once she fell in love, she was certain that she and her partner would settle down in the suburbs, but that hadn't happened. During their twelve-year relationship, she and Judy occasionally discussed buying rather than renting, but they hadn't even gone house-hunting together. Harry didn't know why Judy had resisted, but now that she was getting ready to move to Key West, she was glad that she had never bought a house.

Harry turned as Marg Alexander came in, a gust of cold air following her through the front door. She stood in the spacious foyer, ran her hands through her curly, black hair, and then vigorously rubbed her ears.

"You'd think I would know better," she said with a laugh. "My ears nearly freeze and drop off, but I never could stand wearing a hat."

Harry watched Marg bend down to unlace her boots. "I hate them, too. But my ears get so cold that I feel dizzy when I get inside, so I wear one anyway and worry about my hair later."

Marg stood up and glanced around. When she saw that they were alone, she moved closer to Harry. "Isn't it awful about Julie?"

Harry pursed her lips and nodded.

"It must have been a stranger."

"What? Did you see something the police should know about?"

"Well, no, but who else would have attacked her?"

Harry stared at her. Marg Alexander wasn't stupid. She had been a class leader, both academically and on the playing field. As far as Harry knew, she hadn't lost any of her intelligence since then.

"Who are you trying to fool?"

Marg looked chagrined. "Myself, I guess. I just can't believe that someone we know would use violence to solve a problem."

"Who was having a problem with Julie?"

"Oh, you know what Julie was like," Marg said, her tone deceptively light. She kicked off her lace-up boots and gingerly side-stepped several puddles.

"No, I don't," Harry responded. "Why don't you tell me?"

"Well, she could be a merciless tease, which is no secret to anybody, including you," Marg said, giving Harry a reproachful look. "You were the one she zeroed in on this weekend, after all. I don't have much respect for people who act like that, and Julie was one of the worst. She wasn't a very nice person."

"Did she ever bait you?"

Marg's blue eyes were sharp. "Who hasn't she harassed?"

"You looked upset during the reception the other night," Harry said, changing her line of questioning. "What did Julie say to you?"

"She wasn't coming on to me, if that's what you're insinuating," said Marg.

"I wasn't insinuating anything in particular," Harry said, her tone mild since that was, in fact, precisely what she had been doing. But if Julie hadn't been coming on to Marg, what had she said to upset Marg so much that it had been noticeable across the room? Harry wasn't about to give up, even though Marg was upset with her.

"What *did* Julie say, then?"

"Honestly, Hubbley, sometimes you can be a real pest. What difference does it make what she said to me?"

"If it's not important, why are you so reluctant to tell me?"

Marg flushed. "Do you think that *I* killed Julie? Look, I might have wanted to throttle her at times, as did half the rest of the world, but I never would have actually *hurt* her."

"She could be quite aggravating," Harry agreed.

"So you want to know what she said to me? Well, I'll tell you. Maybe you didn't know this, but Julie was looking for a teaching position in Ontario."

"What?" Harry was flabbergasted. "But she had a good job here. And her house, her relationship with Francine, her —"

Marg held up her hands. "Do you want to hear this or not?"

Harry shut up.

"She called me a little over a year ago and asked if I would keep my eyes open," Marg continued. "Well, the situation in Toronto isn't much better than it is here, what with the government cutbacks in education. But I said I would let her know if anything came up."

"And?"

"Patience wasn't Julie's longest suit. She called nearly every month. I read the want ads and asked around on a regular basis, but there wasn't anything much, a job here, a job there. I gave her the details, but I never asked whether she applied for any. Most positions these days go to teachers who have been laid off by their school board, so there isn't much chance for outsiders."

"It's the same here." Harry was amazed that Julie had seriously considered leaving Quebec. Of course, other than the Lachance sisters, Julie had no close relatives. Her parents had died when she was a child, her father in a boating accident and her mother a lingering death from breast cancer. Apart from some distant cousins who lived in the Gatineau, Julie had been alone in the world. She had claimed not to mind. She had announced that she enjoyed the freedom it gave her and declared that relatives often caused more trouble than they were worth.

"Did she ask you to keep it quiet?"

"Definitely."

"And you did."

"Of course. Why wouldn't I?"

"Why do you think she didn't want anyone to know?" Harry asked.

"Because she didn't want to upset Francine if nothing came of it," replied Marg.

"Do you mean that Francine didn't know?"

"Apparently not," Marg said. "Julie expressly warned me not to say anything to her. I don't know why she bothered, because I've never had a decent conversation with Francine Lachance in my life. I mean, what do you say to a woman who looks like she would rather spit nails than talk?"

Harry smiled absently. She found if difficult to imagine that Julie wouldn't have told Francine about her intentions. Had she planned to mention it to Francine while engaged in casual conversation over dinner one night, or to send a postcard from Toronto? Actually, Harry wouldn't have put it past her. But she still didn't see what that had to do with Marg's irritation with Julie the night of the reception.

"Why were you angry with Julie on Friday evening?"

Marg frowned. "I suppose I should have known better than to tell Julie anything private, but one evening when she called, I was having a lot of pain in my knees and hips. I mentioned that my arthritis was getting worse and that it was making it hard for me to do my job. She made a joke about replacing me when I retired. I didn't think it was very funny. In fact, I was rather taken aback. She glossed over it, and eventually I forgot about what she said. You can imagine my shock when, a couple of weeks later, the head of the department came into the gym with Julie in tow while I was running senior girls' basketball practice."

"You're kidding!"

"No, I'm not. Julie was all hugs and kisses, as if we had always been the best of friends. She professed to be worried about me, concerned about my arthritis, which, of course, was the first time the head of the physical-education department had ever heard about it. My doctor has been closely monitoring my condition, and he knows how much I want to keep on teaching. We have an agreement that I will respect his opinion and stop working when it becomes evident that I'm going to do myself harm. And I haven't reached that point yet. But once Julie made that comment in front of the head of the department, he's been watching me like a hawk and hinting that I should put in for early retirement."

"And the second you did that, Julie would have had your job," Harry surmised.

"I don't know whether there would have to be an open competition or whether they would be compelled to hire a teacher they had previously laid off. As you can imagine, I tried not to think about it," Marg said, an unpleasant edge to her voice. "I never asked if Julie had put in her application — I didn't want to know."

"And Friday night?"

Marg gave Harry a resentful look. "She said she had been told that she had the job, that it was only a matter of time before I would have to leave. And the worst thing was, I didn't know whether to believe her or not."

The door opened and Judy Johnson's head rounded the corner. "Believe who?"

"The tooth fairy," Marg snapped. She hopped over another dirty puddle and strode down the hall.

Leave it to Judy to show up at such a critical moment. There were dozens of questions Harry still wanted to put to Marg. Harry knew that Marg had always been job-proud. She believed in being good at what she did, which meant constantly perfecting her skills and keeping up-to-date on new teaching methods. It was a damn shame that she was going to have to retire early because of a physical disability, and it must have rankled to have Julie not only waiting for her to leave, but also trying to push her out by circulating confidential medical information. The question was, had it rankled enough to provoke Marg to murder?

Judy stepped into the foyer and closed the front door. "She's certainly got a flea up her ass, hasn't she?"

"It would seem so."

Judy's thick, dark hair was windblown and her cheeks were rosy from the cold. She unzipped her jacket, hung it on the doorknob and kicked off her knee-high leather boots.

"Where's Sarah?"

Judy pulled a pair of black penny loafers from the corduroy shoebag dangling from her shoulder, tossed them on the floor and stepped into them. "She didn't feel like coming."

Not wanting to pass up the opportunity to question Judy, Harry followed her ex-lover from the vestibule, her self-appointed and rather informal job of brunch hostess all but forgotten in her rush to prevent Judy from reaching the living room. She reached out and grasped Judy's arm.

"We've got to talk."

"After last night, I haven't got anything to say to you."

"Don't be silly." Harry moved closer. She was going to lose her if she didn't think of something to get her attention, and quick. "At least tell me how long you and Julie Beliveau were lovers," she said.

Judy looked as if she had been sucker punched. "Who told you?" she hissed, grabbing Harry's shoulders. "WHO TOLD YOU? Who would want to bring that up again after all these years?"

Bingo! Harry closed her hands around Judy's wrists and removed her hands from her shoulders.

"Who do you think?"

"That bitch!" Judy fumed.

Which one, Harry wondered, waiting for Judy to mention her by name.

"But why would she say anything to you?"

Harry shrugged.

"Listen, we can't talk here. Someone might hear." Judy slid into her jacket and walked swiftly toward the front door. "Let's go outside."

"But it's cold out there," Harry protested.

"Do you want to talk or not?"

Harry's boots were hidden somewhere under the pile heaped on the grey rubber boot tray. She tossed salt-stained boots aside and found hers on the bottom. They were wet, but she slipped them on anyway, although she didn't attempt to do up the greasy-looking laces.

"Wait," she said to Judy, who had already opened the front door.

"I haven't got all day."

Harry opened the door to the closet and retrieved her leather jacket. Thank goodness she had arrived early enough to find space in the closet. If she'd had to excavate her jacket from the bed in the spare room, she would have lost this opportunity to question Judy about her involvement with Julie Beliveau. Harry pulled on her hat and wrapped her scarf around her neck.

"Are you finally ready?" Judy gave her a disdainful look and left. Harry followed, bracing for the cold. But the wind had nearly died down, and it wasn't as bad as she had imagined it would be. Judy led her down the concrete staircase. "Let's go over there."

They stood beside the bulky staircase. It completely cut the wind and hid them from view. Harry retrieved her gloves from the pockets of her leather jacket and slipped them on.

"Sue shouldn't have told you," Judy whispered angrily. "It was confidential, between the two of us."

So it had been Sue Phillips who had known about Judy and Julie Beliveau's affair. She had also known about Manon and Julie's relationship. What a veritable well of information Phillips was. Perhaps Harry should question her about the others. If Sue was still speaking to her, that is.

"How on earth did she find out?"

"The same way anybody unearths a secret in this community of ours. It's nearly impossible to keep anything private for long. Julie and I ran into Sue in one of the bars on Ste-Catherine," Judy replied. "It's ironic, isn't it? You know how I've always hated bars, but since Julie and I both lived with other women, we had no where else to go."

A chill passed through Harry, and it wasn't from the cold weather. "How long ago was this?"

Something in Harry's voice caught Judy's attention. The cautious look which appeared on her face gave Harry the answer to her question. She sighed with disgust.

"Come on, Harry, you know what Julie was like. She was just coming off a relationship and she was in the mood to fool around. And you and

I hadn't been together all that long. We were still getting used to each other when Julie came on to me. It was sort of a last fling for me, at least in the beginning."

How could Judy have betrayed her like that? Harry reflected angrily. They had been so much in love. And why hadn't she known? Was she really that unobservant? "That's your excuse?"

Judy tilted her head and gave a curt laugh. "I don't really need one now, do I?"

The more she learned, the more inclined Harry was to believe that Judy had never been monogamous during the twelve years they had spent together. But she was afraid to ask; she wasn't yet willing to admit to herself that Judy had lied to her, not once or twice, but continuously.

"How right you are," Harry said through gritted teeth. If she lost her temper, Judy would go into a huff and stop talking. "You were telling me?"

"I used to pretend that I had to work late," Judy continued. "We normally went to one of those cheap motels over on Taschereau in Brossard, but one night I didn't have time. I don't remember why, but we only had a few hours. That's why we went to that stupid bar. We were certain that no one we knew ever frequented that particular club."

Harry began pacing. "And Sue was there."

"Yes, wouldn't you know it? She and some of the other gay teachers in her school were out slumming that night. She took one look at the two of us together and that was it. Once Sue found out about our affair, Julie ended it. I was afraid that Sue would tell you, but apparently she never did."

Harry wasn't sure whether she was pleased or sorry that Sue hadn't spilled the beans. She stopped pacing and gave Judy a penetrating glance.

"Why did you get involved with Julie in the first place?"

"Because she was there and she wanted me."

Harry leaned all her weight on one foot in an attempt to defrost the bottom of the other.

"If you utter so much as one judgmental word, I swear that I'll never speak to you again as long as I live," Judy said vehemently.

Harry said nothing.

"If you had been able to cope with my need to retain a certain amount of independence, it might have been different. Why do you think I didn't tell you about these things while they were going on?"

How about, because they were wrong? Harry thought. She skulked in the corner and kept her mouth shut.

"We both know it finally reached the point that I couldn't hide things from you any longer. And what happened then? As soon as I got involved with Sarah, all you did was climb on your high horse and criticize. I could accept that you wanted to be monogamous, but you could never deal with the fact that I didn't. If you had only left me alone instead of doing all that moralizing, we might still be together."

Moralize? Who, her? Well, yes; Judy was right. Harry moralized right down to her booties, and there was not a damn thing she could do about it. It was in her genes. Not that that should have made any difference; Judy shouldn't have lied to her. If she had known right from the beginning that Judy wanted to be in a non-monogamous relationship, she likely wouldn't have committed herself the way she had.

But that was water under the bridge, and Harry didn't want to get involved in a discussion about who was to blame for the end of their relationship. As far as she was concerned, it was Judy's fault. She cleared her throat. "I take it you didn't want Julie to break up with you."

Judy didn't reply.

"You weren't in love with her, were you?"

Judy turned away, her voice bitter. "Go ahead and laugh."

Harry couldn't believe it. They had barely started to live together, and not only had Judy cheated on her, she had also fallen in love with Julie. Why hadn't Harry noticed? Had she been in love with love, infatuated with a mirage?

"You're not laughing."

"No, and I don't intend to." Twelve years of her life had just gone down the tubes. She was angry with her ex-lover, but she also pitied her, as she would anyone who became obsessed with a woman like Julie.

"I didn't plan to fall in love," Judy said, her voice low. "It was just one of those things."

There was such a thing as self-control, wasn't there? And what would have happened if Julie hadn't ended their relationship? Would Judy had left her?

"I don't believe this," Harry sputtered.

"I didn't think you would ever find out. In the end, you left anyway, and —"

"Wait a minute!" Harry interrupted. "You were the one who walked out on me, not the other way around!"

"Physically, Harry, physically," replied Judy in a tired voice. "But emotionally you were gone a long time before I moved out."

But that was because Judy was involved with Sarah. Harry was so upset that she couldn't think straight. She hated it when history got revised, especially her own.

"Actually, Sue didn't tell me about you and Julie."

"Then how did you find out?"

"Someone saw the way you were looking at Julie at the bar Friday night," Harry said. "Apparently it was just a few hours before she was murdered."

"Shortly after I moved in with Sarah, I began wondering whether I had made the right decision," Judy mused aloud.

Why was she telling Harry this *now*? To distract her? She leaned against the brick wall and stared at Judy. She looked so familiar, and yet essentially she was a stranger.

"I knew that my relationship with you was well and truly over, but I started to question the wisdom of living with someone else so soon," Judy explained. "To be truthful, I feel smothered, but I'm not doing anything about it because I don't want to be alone."

"Look, Judy, I really don't want to hear about this. You were seen talking to Julie the night she died —"

"You mean that I'm a suspect simply because she and I were having a little chat? Is that what you're trying to say? Don't be silly. Even you've got more sense than that. Julie talked to dozens of women that night, you included."

"It was *how* you were looking at her."

"Oh, and I suppose you've got a photograph of the expression on my face?" Judy taunted.

Harry no longer had the energy to be angry. "You're twisting my words."

"What do you want to know? Whether I was still in love with her?"

Harry nodded.

"You're such a fool, Harry. But if you must know, Julie and I never got together again while you and I were lovers."

Harry closed her eyes. There was something purifying about the cold which was seeping into her bones. She concentrated on that instead of what Judy was saying.

"I didn't see her much of her over the years."

"And there were other distractions," Harry commented, her voice dry.

"I'll pretend I didn't hear that."

Do that, Harry thought.

"Then Sarah and I were invited to a party at Manon and Sue's. It was this past summer, and you were away, so I guess they thought it was safe. I used to be friends with them, but that was the first time they called after you and I broke up. I hate it when people drop you from their lives after a relationship is over. Anyway, Sarah and I went to their party. Julie was there. She was by herself — Francine was working at l'Entr'acte that night. Julie flirted outrageously with me."

"And?"

"You don't understand that kind of sexual attraction, do you?"

Perhaps not. Or maybe she did. After fifty years, she still hadn't managed to get into another woman's libido, and she likely never would. Anyway, wasn't sensuality relative? What Harry actually understood was that Judy had never felt that way about her.

"Julie made me feel like a million dollars, especially sexually."

Harry was in a no-win situation. The more she compared herself to Julie, the more inadequate she felt. She had to get a grip; she and Judy were no longer lovers, and Julie was dead.

"So what were you talking about Friday night at the bar?"

"That's none of your business."

"Did you ask her to go out with you?" Harry persevered.

"Hell, yes. What you do think? After she flirted with me at Manon and Sue's, I wanted to start seeing her again. I phoned her several times at school, but she never returned my calls. After a couple of weeks, she left a message for me at work, telling me in no uncertain terms to leave her alone. Apparently the people in the office were getting annoyed."

"Did you stop calling her?"

"Of course," Judy said. "What else could I do? I didn't dare phone her at home. Francine would have been suspicious. So I did my best to get over her."

"But you didn't succeed," Harry surmised.

"No, I didn't."

Judy sounded miserable, but Harry had no time for compassion.

"And you never convinced her to date you again."

"When I approached her Friday night, she told me that there was someone else, that, compared to this woman, I was boring. *Boring!* No one has *ever* called me that before."

Even though Julie Beliveau was dead, Judy's anger was still palpable. Julie had scorned her, something unforgivable for someone who possessed so much pride. It was then that Harry started to think that Judy, a woman she had known and loved for so many years, might actually have murdered someone.

"So you were mad enough to kill her," Harry said, her voice soft.

Judy wheeled around and glared at Harry. "Yes. But I didn't."

Harry had no sooner returned to the house and removed her boots and leather jacket than someone began knocking forcefully on the front door.

"It's unlocked," she shouted.

The rapping continued. Harry hung her jacket in the closet and then opened the front door. In the process, she soaked her socks in cold, slushy water, which annoyed her. She hated having wet feet.

Lieutenant-Detective Claude Gagnon loomed in the doorway, as big as the light of day. He was taller and stockier than Harry remembered.

"Ah — *bonjour*, Madame Hubbley."

"*Bonjour*." Harry casually reached behind her and pulled the inside door shut.

The detective frowned. "What's going on in there?"

Harry wished she could warn her friends, most of whom had likely imbibed enough champagne to be a bit too voluble for comfort, especially with a policeman on the premises. "Perhaps no one explained to you that this brunch is part of the teachers' convention."

Gagnon raised his bushy eyebrows. "Perhaps not," he eventually said. "But I do believe that Manon Lachance lives here, and that she's the twin sister of Francine Lachance, who lived with Julie Beliveau, who, as we both know, was murdered last night."

"Well, yes," Harry prevaricated, although she hadn't seen Manon and Sue since she arrived earlier that morning, before eleven as promised, much to Raven's chagrin. Manon looked tired, as if she hadn't slept at all, and Sue had a pinched expression on her face. There were wrinkles around Manon's eyes and mouth that Harry had never noticed before. One of her lovers was dead, but Manon couldn't mourn in public. Sue also looked tired and defeated. Knowing what Sue had already been through in her long relationship with Manon, Harry wouldn't have been surprised if she had finally run out of patience. After letting Harry and Raven in, both women had returned to the family room and left Harry in charge.

The detective impatiently shifted from one foot to another. He fumbled in his coat pocket, pulled a pack of cigarettes from one pocket and a silver-plated lighter from another, and lit up without asking Harry's permission. She wasn't surprised. It happened all the time in Montreal, and not just with cops.

"*Écoutez*," he said firmly after he took a long drag on his cigarette. "Listen. I know you want to protect your friends, but somebody killed her, after all. And face it," he shrugged, "it was likely one of them."

It didn't take long for the vestibule to fill with cigarette smoke. Harry's nose began to run. "So?" she croaked, searching through her pockets for a tissue. She sneezed before she could find one, and he stepped back to escape the line of fire. "Sorry," she said with a sniff, although she really wasn't. "I'm allergic to cigarette smoke."

"Not only could it have been one of your friends, it could have been you," he said, taking another deep drag and flicking ashes on the floor.

Harry didn't dignify his comment with a reply. "Who in particular do you want to see?"

The detective raised the corner of his mouth; Harry supposed that was his version of a smile. "Everyone who was there that night."

Harry stood her ground. Other than the policewoman who had taken her to bed in Provincetown a couple of years ago, she always seemed to have bad luck with cops. "Does it have to be right now?"

"I'm here, aren't I?"

"So am I, so why don't you start with me?"

Lieutenant-Detective Gagnon dropped his cigarette butt on the floor. It sizzled in a dirty puddle and went out. Not only had he never learned how to smile, he also hadn't been taught proper manners. Or perhaps he was trying to intimidate her. The tension between them increased. It made Harry feel like stretching, but she resisted the impulse. Instead, she crossed her arms and leaned against a wall.

He crossed his arms and leaned against the opposite wall. Harry's respect for him sank to the level of the dirty puddle in which his extinguished cigarette butt was wallowing.

"I hear that you and Madame Beliveau were having an affair," he remarked.

For an opening salvo, that wasn't great. Harry was perversely disappointed in him. "You heard wrong. Julie Beliveau enjoyed flirting, but so do a lot of people."

He gave an elaborate shrug and his broad shoulders seemed to fill the doorway. "That's the gossip," he commented, lighting another cigarette.

Harry refused to be provoked. Instead, she sneezed twice in rapid succession, and then said, "Gossip is quite amusing, of course. But if I were you, I wouldn't put much stock in it. I certainly wouldn't base my findings in a murder case on mere hearsay."

"You would say that, especially if you killed Madame Beliveau."

Harry was spared the necessity of replying when the front door abruptly opened. It slammed into the detective's back and knocked him against the closet door. She stifled a grin as he grunted and moved out of the way of further damage.

"Oh! It's you!" Isabelle Lachance exclaimed once she had slid inside the vestibule and inspected the cowering Gagnon. "What are you doing here, anyway? Do you have to bother us in our hour of grief? I'm going to complain to the civilian review board about your behaviour, you can be sure about that! Harriet, has he been mistreating you? I'm sure he has, just from the expression on his face. He has absolutely no mercy for those in grief, does he? Well, let me tell you, Monsieur Lieutenant-Detective, you have met your match in me and my husband! We're respectable civil servants, just like you. I'm tired of being harassed, and your superiors are going to hear about it. So why don't you remove your official carcass from these premises and let us mourn in peace?"

"But there's a party going on in there," Gagnon sputtered. He dropped his cigarette butt on the floor. This one missed the puddle, so he pressed the toe of his boot into it and crushed it.

Isabelle drew herself up to her official height of five-foot-one-and-a-half and glared at the cop. "You listen to me, *monsieur*; we of the Lachance family grieve in our own way, and who are you to question how that is? A member of our family has been killed, and we are having our own private wake. Now, unless you have a warrant for someone's arrest or to enter this house, get out! And take your filthy cigarettes with you!"

Harry nearly swooned; why could she never speak to a cop that way?

Lieutenant-Detective Gagnon seemed to shrink in stature. He defiantly lit a cigarette and then opened the front door.

"I'll be back, and you're the first one I'm going to see," he said pointedly to Isabelle Lachance. "And you'll be the second," he added, glaring at Harry. He left the vestibule, slamming the door behind him.

Isabelle flipped the lock, cocked her head and grinned at Harry. "He's a real bastard, isn't he?"

"*Oui*," Harry replied weakly.

"He came by our house early this morning and roused Albert and me from bed," Isabelle said. "Perhaps he thought he would get something from us if we were half asleep, but it was just the opposite; we clammed up and told him nothing."

Harry nodded.

"Not that there was anything to tell him," Isabelle added swiftly. "But even if there had been, we wouldn't have said a word. We Lachances react that way to government officials like him, whether they wear a badge or not. Nobody's going to make us say something we don't want to. But, then, aren't all families that way?"

"I suppose so," Harry said. The vestibule was getting cold, so she opened the inner door.

"Ah, yes, I forgot: You're an only child, aren't you? But never mind. You can imagine how it is among close siblings. Anyway, that's not important. We got rid of that officious bastard, didn't we?" She looked into the house. "Where's Manon?"

"Somewhere in there," Harry replied. "Listen, Isabelle, you told me that you and Albert were at a bistro on St-Denis Saturday evening, nearly across the street from l'Entr'acte."

"That's right."

"And you were with friends the whole time?"

Isabelle looked impatient. "*Oui*."

"Do you mean that neither of you ever went to the bathroom?"

Isabelle frowned. "Don't get cute. And show some loyalty to the family, will you? Besides, why would Albert or I want to kill Julie?"

"I was hoping you could tell me that. What was Julie holding over you?" Harry retorted, taking a shot in the dark. People who protested too much always roused her curiosity.

The anger drained from Isabelle's face. "What makes you think she was holding anything over us?"

"I think you know the answer to that," Harry bluffed.

Isabelle looked indecisive, but just for a split second. "I don't know what you're talking about." She pushed past Harry and went into the house.

It had been a worth a try, Harry reflected. At least now she knew that either Isabelle or Albert had a secret involving Julie Beliveau. She followed Isabelle into the hall.

"Where have you been?" Elizabeth Martin gushed when Harry entered the crowded living room. When Liz wrapped her arms around her and gave her an effusive hug, Harry realized that she was drunk.

"Around," Harry responded with a wary laugh.

Marg Alexander and Sophie Lister were in the living room, but they were talking to each other and didn't notice Harry. She gently removed Liz's arms from her neck and backed out of the room. Isabelle Lachance was nowhere in sight. Harry pushed her way through the packed dining room and into the kitchen. The counters were littered with discarded champagne and empty two-litre soft-drink bottles, abandoned styrofoam coffee cups, and hors d'oeuvre trays which had been emptied of everything except wilted lettuce leaves and sprigs of parsley.

Harry opened the fridge and retrieved a lone bottle of champagne partially hidden behind a carton of milk. Then she searched through the cupboards until she found a wine glass. She grasped the bottle of champagne in one hand and the wine glass in the other.

Albert Dack burst into the kitchen. "Where's my wife?"

Harry protectively clutched the bottle of champagne to her breast. "I don't know. Have you tried the living room?"

"Everybody's drunk."

"How about the dining room?"

Albert rubbed his bald head with his hand. "She's not there. Dammit, you must have followed the same route through the house I did."

Harry rolled her eyes.

Albert gave her a disgusted look and bolted from the kitchen.

He was a strange man, Harry mused, relaxing her grasp on her bottle of champagne. And an obsessed one, too. Did he really think that some lesbian was going to seduce his wife if he didn't stick to her like glue every time they went to one of her sister's social gatherings?

Harry removed the foil from the tip of the bottle, eased out the cork and filled the wine glass with champagne. She leaned against the counter and sipped from her glass, thinking that she was getting nowhere fast. Or perhaps that wasn't quite right; she was getting somewhere, but she had yet to figure out where. Right now she was more confused than anything else. What were Isabelle Lachance and Albert Dack hiding? Had Julie been blackmailing them? And if so, about what?

Sue Phillips entered the kitchen. She had on her winter coat, and her purse was slung over a shoulder. "So here you are. Sophie told me that she thought you had come this way. I thought you might already be downstairs."

"So that's where Manon is," Harry remarked, relieved that Sue was once again talking to her. Not many people knew about Manon and Sue's family room because they generally entertained all but close friends in their living room.

"Yes. At least she was in the family room the last time I saw her," Sue said with a nod. "Listen, could you put me up for a few days?"

Harry's chin dropped.

"No, I take that back; it's not a good idea, not with Raven staying with you."

"It's just that so much of my stuff is packed. But there's a trundle bed in my office, and you could use that if you don't mind being surrounded by boxes," Harry added hastily.

"Never mind," Sue said decisively. "I'll give my sister a call. She won't mind if I take up residence in their spare room for a few nights."

"What about Manon?" Harry asked quietly.

Sue pushed one of the empty trays aside and dumped her purse on the counter. "Are you planning to finish off that bottle all by yourself?"

"Of course not," Harry said automatically. She took another wine glass from the cupboard, filled it with champagne and handed it to Sue.

"You think I'm being insensitive, don't you?" Sue asked once she had half emptied her glass. She sat it beside her purse and looked directly at Harry.

"I'm not sure," Harry answered, and it was the truth. She stared back at Sue. "Just after Julie was killed, you told me that you knew that Manon and Julie had been seeing each other. But you wouldn't say how long you knew about it, and neither would Manon."

Sue finished her glass of champagne. "So?"

"You didn't find out until last night, did you?"

"What are you talking about?" Sue scoffed. She reached for the bottle and refilled her glass. "I've known for a long time."

"I don't think so," Harry said.

Sue made an impatient gesture and picked up her purse.

Harry put her hand on Sue's arm to prevent her from leaving. "Why did you call me from the bar and then put Francine on the phone?"

"We were just trying to find out where you were," responded Sue.

"But what difference did it make? And why did Francine immediately accuse me of being with Julie?"

"Oh, come on — you know the answer to that. Julie had been flirting with you all weekend."

"But people didn't go to the bar in a group. Some of them went to move their cars into parking lots, others went for coffee," Harry insisted. "And I didn't even show up for dinner on Prince-Arthur. So why did Francine assume Julie was with me?"

Sue looked sullen. "How do I know?"

"You told her, didn't you?"

"Come off it, Harry — you're dreaming in technicolour," Sue said with a false laugh.

"I don't think so."

"Why would I do a stupid thing like that?"

"Because something happened over the weekend to make you realize that Manon and Julie were lovers." Harry held up her hand to prevent Sue from speaking. "I'm right, aren't I?"

There was a long silence and then Sue folded. "Yes," she whispered.

"What gave them away?"

"I watched them play one-on-one during the pick-up basketball game, and everything suddenly fell into place," Sue responded.

"The way they fooled around, you mean?"

"Not really. I never thought anything about their bantering and teasing. They had done that since they met. It was how their bodies seemed so in sync when they ran up and down the floor. They looked like they had played on the same team every day of their lives," Sue answered.

"And when you confronted Manon with your knowledge, she admitted it."

"It didn't happen quite that way," Sue said.

"What do you mean?"

"She told me the next evening. I was mulling things over because I couldn't live with the knowledge that Manon and Julie were lovers. It was eating at my insides. I knew I would have to make her confess and then break up with Julie. But in the end, she surprised me. Manon is a moral coward any which way you want to define it, but she doesn't lie. If you catch her, she'll tell you the truth. In this case, she owned up before I had decided what to do," Sue said, her voice bitter.

"Did she realize that you already knew?"

"No. And there was no point in telling her then."

"So when Francine started asking questions about Julie, you threw her off the track by joking about how Julie had been coming on to me."

Sue nodded.

"But why?"

"Because I was ambivalent about Francine finding out about their affair," responded Sue. "I knew she would be angry, and I was concerned about what would happen between her and Manon."

"Were you afraid that she would react violently?"

"How the hell would I know precisely how she would react?" Sue said testily. "I just didn't want to be responsible for Manon and Francine having a total bust-up and never speaking to each other again."

"Didn't you think Francine would find out anyway?"

"It took me two years to discover that Manon and Julie were lovers," said Sue. "Maybe it would have taken Francine another two years. Or perhaps she might never have found out. Who knows?"

"And now you're leaving."

"I can't stay," averred Sue. "Too much has happened."

"You've left her before and gone back again."

"You don't have to remind me. But this time it's over for good."

Harry wondered about that, but she didn't say anything.

Sue finished her champagne and put her glass on the counter. "I've got to go."

"You can come back to my place," Harry offered swiftly.

"There's no way I'm going to stay with someone who thinks I killed Julie." Sue's voice bubbled over with emotion. She turned and rushed from the kitchen.

There was that, Harry thought glumly. The problem was, every darn one of them was a suspect.

Harry had another half-glass of champagne, picked up the bottle and left the kitchen. She slipped through the dining room and down the stairs into the basement.

"So here you are." Harry pushed through the swinging doors and into the family room. She put her half-empty bottle of champagne on the large, oval wood coffee table that was positioned between the two sofas.

"Yeah. Here we are, hiding out from the world," Manon responded. She sounded drunk. She was sprawled on a three-seat sofa covered in faded brown and beige material. Her sister Isabelle was perched on the same sofa, and from the stern expression on her face, it looked as if Isabelle had been chewing out Manon. A big-screen television was blaring in the far corner of the room. A National Football League game was on. Albert was seated on a two-seat sofa covered with the same nubby material, watching the game. Raven was sitting in an old recliner. Her eyes were closed, but Harry didn't think that she was asleep.

Harry walked over to Manon and Isabelle and sat on the arm of the sofa. "Am I interrupting something?"

"We were discussing Julie's death," Manon responded.

"Don't let me stop you," Harry said.

Manon stood up. "Where did you find that bottle? I thought they had finished the champagne long ago."

"It was in the fridge," Harry replied. She watched Manon fill her glass.

"Aren't you supposed to be the official greeting party?"

"They don't need one at this point," Harry said.

Manon drained her glass and filled it again. Harry wondered how she could drink champagne so rapidly without having to burp.

"Just as long as they don't steal the silver." Manon carried the bottle and her glass back to the sofa and sat down beside her sister, holding the bottle on one knee and the wine glass on the other.

Harry had hoped that she would be able to question the Lachance sisters, but Manon was obviously drunk, and Isabelle wasn't making her feel all that welcome. She looked across the room at Raven, who opened her eyes and winked. What on earth did that mean? Raven shut her eyes again before Harry could respond.

Everyone suddenly grew interested in what was on television. Harry turned toward the big screen just in time to see several helmeted football players down an opponent, then fall on top of him. This was followed by a lot of high-fiving and bum patting. Football was not her favourite sport, and not just because she had never played it. And she was certain it wasn't the Lachance sisters' game of choice, either. She knew when she was being shut out.

She sighed and stood up. "Are you ready to go?" she asked Raven.

"So soon?" Isabelle inquired with faux politeness.

Harry felt annoyed. She looked at Manon, who was trying to stifle a grin, but she was too drunk to do a very successful job.

"You should take this seriously," Harry said. "Lieutenant-Detective Gagnon is hot of the trail of Julie Beliveau's killer, and he's no fool."

Isabelle Lachance bounced to her feet. "Are you accusing my sister —"

"Did I say anything to make you think that?" Harry interrupted.

Isabelle sank back on the sofa, a frown on her face. Albert was making funny noises under his breath. At first Harry thought he was swearing at her, perhaps in defence of his wife, who, in Harry's opinion, didn't need his help. Then she realized that Albert had fallen asleep and was snoring lightly.

"I'm not jumping to conclusions, but the detective might," Harry said.

Manon stirred. "What are you trying to say?"

"Lieutenant-Detective Gagnon thinks that the person who killed Julie was a close friend. A *very* close friend."

"And you?" Isabelle asked, her voice sharp. "What do you think?"

Harry ran through various responses, but none was adequate.

"Hell, she probably suspects all of us," Manon remarked, pouring the last of the champagne into her wine glass. Harry had hoped to have more, but she no longer cared. Champagne hangovers were among the worst.

It was then that Raven spoke up. "Well, it's clear that someone killed Julie Beliveau."

"Who asked you?" Isabelle interjected none too kindly.

Harry headed toward the door. It was time to leave. "Come on, Raven. I've got packing to do, and a full week of school ahead of me. Besides, they want to be alone."

Raven got up, stretched and sauntered across the braided rug which covered most of the floor.

"By the way, Sue *isn't* staying at my place this time," Harry added.

"WHAT?"

"You didn't know?" Harry said as Raven linked her arm through Harry's and leaned against her.

"SHE WHAT?"

"You can reach her at her sister's," Harry added as they left.

It was five o'clock in the afternoon when she and Raven got off the bus at the corner of avenue du Parc and avenue Mont-Royal. Harry was exhausted. She felt as if she could sleep for a month.

"You need a good meal," Raven lectured as they took a short-cut through Fletcher's Field and came out just beside the tennis courts.

Raven was right; Harry hadn't had anything except a glass and a half of champagne for brunch.

"I'll rustle up something," Raven added.

Oh, to be young again, Harry reflected, although she was certain that there was nothing of nutritional value in her fridge or her cupboards. She walked slowly up the stairs while Raven went on ahead, taking the snow-covered steps two at a time. Just before she reached the top, she stopped suddenly and turned to face Harry.

"What's the matter?"

"Your front door is open," Raven replied, placing a cautionary hand on Harry's arm.

Harry was certain she hadn't left it that way. Her door had to be locked from the outside, and she had closed it behind her and turned around and stuck her key in the lock so many times that it was now second nature.

"I know I locked it."

"I remember you doing it," Raven agreed.

Harry pushed past Raven. She didn't have all that many material possessions, especially since she had given into Judy's demands for many of the appliances and the best of the furniture they had purchased together, but the thought that someone had broken in made her shudder.

"Don't you dare go in there!" Raven admonished.

"But I have to see —"

"It's too dangerous, and you know it."

Raven was right. The burglar could still be in her apartment. Harry took a step backwards. Her cosy home suddenly felt dangerous, and she was furious.

"We can call the police from the *dépanneur* on Parc."

"The what?"

"Convenience store," Harry said impatiently. She wanted to barge into her apartment and beat the shit out of the intruder, but, instead, she turned and rushed down the steps. As she ran back through Fletcher's Field, she could hear Raven stumbling behind her.

"Wait," Raven puffed.

"Hurry up."

Harry grasped Raven's hand and they swiftly crossed avenue du Parc and entered the convenience store on the corner. Harry pulled off her hat, removed the receiver from the pay phone and dialled 911. She reported the break-in and was transferred to the desk sergeant of the local precinct, whose interest noticeably flagged when Harry asked that the information be passed onto Lieutenant-Detective Gagnon. He promised to send a squad car and to notify the detective, but Harry didn't believe him.

"Let's go," she said to Raven.

"They're going to send someone?"

"Your guess is as good as mine."

"No, but they are, right?"

"I think so," Harry replied as they left the convenience store. "They don't always, sometimes they tell you to make a list of what's missing and take it to your local police station. But I think they'll show up in this case. I told the sergeant that the burglar might still be in my apartment."

"That will do it every time."

A police car with its lights flashing pulled up in front of her triplex just as Harry and Raven returned. The car door opened and a tall, big-boned policewoman unfolded her limbs from the driver's seat.

"I'm Officer Roche and my partner is Officer Caron. Are you the one who called?" she asked Harry.

"Yes."

Officer Roche fumbled through her notebook. "Madame Hubbley, right?"

"That's right. I think someone broke into my apartment. It's the one upstairs," Harry said, pointing toward her door.

"You haven't cleared the snow yet," the policewoman growled.

"I've been busy," Harry replied.

The cop gave her a that's-what-they-all-say look while unsnapping her holster. "The door looks closed to me."

"I was all the way to the top of the staircase, officer, and the door was definitely open," Raven interjected. "About this much, approximately," she added, spreading her hands a foot wide. "Maybe there was someone inside when we first got here. Perhaps the intruder left while we were in the store using the phone, and shut the door behind them."

Office Roche turned toward her partner, a short, compactly built man with a thick moustache. "Let's see what it's all about, then," she said, sounding resigned.

He nodded and they hurried up the steps.

"Come on," Raven said to Harry.

"Maybe we had better wait down here."

"Why?"

Harry watched Raven climb the stairs and then reluctantly followed.

"You should have stayed on the sidewalk," Officer Roche said.

"It's her apartment," Raven pointed out.

The policewoman gave Raven a dirty look. "At least stand back. You don't want to get hurt if there's trouble."

Harry pulled Raven aside. "She's right."

The police officers drew their service revolvers and stood to either side of the door. Officer Roche reached out, closed her gloved hand around the doorknob and slowly turned it.

"It's not locked," she whispered to her partner in French.

"It's open," Harry translated for Raven's benefit.

Raven nodded absently, her attention on the police officers.

Officer Caron threw open the door, and the two constables stormed Harry's apartment. There was a lot of noise followed by silence.

Raven looked at Harry. "Should we go in?"

"Let's wait for them to come back. They're nervous enough without us getting in the way." Harry rubbed her freezing ears. She had left her woollen hat on top of the telephone in the convenience store, but there was no point in going back to retrieve it. Someone would have taken it by now. She had several others, but they were all in the hall closet.

It seemed like forever, but in reality it was only a couple of minutes before the two police officers returned to the porch. Officer Roche came out first, her revolver once again secured in its holster. She had a frown on her face.

Harry stepped forward.

"You were right. Somebody broke in," the policewoman said.

Officer Caron paused in the doorway to inspect the lock and the doorjamb. "Looks as if he used a small crowbar or a large screwdriver. He jammed it between the door and the frame and forced the door open. The lock might be okay, but it's not going to be much good until you get the frame repaired."

"The place looks a little messy," Officer Roche said. "I take it you're getting ready to move."

Harry nodded. "Yes."

"There's a lot of stuff spread around," said Officer Caron. "Are you in the habit of leaving messages for yourself on the bathroom mirror?"

"What?"

Officer Roche opened her notebook. "It's written with lipstick and it says 'Stop asking questions.'"

"Got any idea what that means?" asked Officer Caron.

"No," Harry lied.

Neither of the police officers looked surprised.

"Well, if anything comes to mind, let us know. I'll get a report form from my car. You can fill it out and bring it down to the station once you've figured out whether anything is missing," the policewoman said with a blunt nod.

"I would get this fixed right away, if I were you," the male officer added, tapping the gouged doorjamb.

"I will," said Harry. She watched the two police officers make their way down the stairs.

"That's *it?*" asked Raven.

Harry turned and glanced into her apartment, but she didn't go inside. She preferred to wait until the police had left before discovering for herself what "a little messy" meant.

"I guess so."

"Memories of home," joked Raven. "There are so many burglaries that they're hardly considered a crime anymore. Unless somebody gets hurt, that is." She put her arm around Harry's waist and gave her a protective hug.

"Yeah," Harry responded half-heartedly. Although she had been a big-city dweller for most of her adult life, this was the first time her home had been broken into. Was this really related to Julie's death in some way? What else could such a message mean?

Officer Roche bounced up the stairs and handed Harry several printed forms. "Fill these out as soon as you can."

Harry nodded.

"Not that you're likely to get your stuff back, you understand. But we do our best," the policewoman hastened to say.

Harry supposed that this was as much sympathy as she was going to get from the police, who undoubtedly saw this sort of thing and worse every day. It might be different if the two officers knew she was involved in a recent murder investigation, but she wasn't going to tell them that. She folded the forms and stuffed them in the pocket of her leather jacket. Office Roche nodded, this time rather warmly, Harry thought, and ran back down the stairs.

"So," Raven said, glancing uncertainly at Harry.

Harry grimaced. "So." She took Raven's hand in hers, stepped over the threshold and trod resolutely into her apartment. The police had turned on the lights in every room, and the vandalism was obvious. Everything had been turned upside down; boxes she had so meticulously packed had been opened, their contents spilled on the floor. Her precious books, some of which she had owned since childhood, were scattered helter-skelter throughout the house. Some of their spines were broken, as if they had been walked on.

As they took stock, Raven uprighted chairs which had been knocked over. Every bedroom dresser drawer had been emptied. Underwear, pairs of socks and tee-shirts littered the floor. Clothes had been pulled wholesale from her closet and spread randomly throughout the apartment, most of their hangers still in place.

Raven went into the bathroom while Harry rushed into the kitchen, anxious to see whether it had been wrecked. More books were strewn on the floor and some of her clothes were draped over the table, but the cupboards and drawers hadn't been touched. Why had the vandal chosen not to destroy the kitchen? Her dishes were still stacked in the cupboards, and what little food there was remained in the fridge. Had the thief heard Raven on the stairs and decided to scram before the police arrived?

"Harry, come see the message the cops were talking about," Raven called.

Harry snapped out of a daze and hurried into the bathroom, her mind still on the rather pristine state of the kitchen. There were clothes in the bathtub, and toilet paper was festooned everywhere, but the medicine cabinet hadn't been emptied. Printed on the mirror in blood-red lipstick were the words: **STOP ASKING QUESTIONS!**

"Well," Harry said, her calm tone of voice belying the agitated state of her nerves.

"I don't imagine that you're going to quit, are you?"

"Of course not."

Raven gathered up some toilet paper from the bathtub. "The nerve of that bastard, using my lipstick. Shall I wipe it off, then?"

Harry was certain that Lieutenant-Detective Gagnon would pay her a visit sooner or later, whether the desk sergeant passed on her message or not. There would be a report of the break-in, of the message written on her mirror, and someone would put two and two together. Did she want to leave the writing there until then? She stared at the mirror. The printing was scrawled, as if the person who wrote it was in a hurry. Was this a last-minute gesture or had the person planned the break-in around it?

"Harriet?"

Lieutenant-Detective Gagnon would take a much closer look at her. He would want to know why she was asking questions. If he decided to have her watched, or worse, put a tail on her, she wouldn't be able to continue her investigations. Erasing it wouldn't stop him from putting pressure on her. But she certainly didn't want to stare at it every time she looked at herself in the mirror.

"Get rid of it," she said.

Raven set to with a vengeance and, seconds later, the warning was gone. She stuffed the red toilet paper into the garbage can and washed her hands.

"That takes care of that," she said harshly. "I'm worried, though. It could be dangerous for you to keep prying into their affairs."

"Maybe. Still, it could have been worse," Harry replied. "They could have really trashed the place." She gathered up the rest of the toilet paper and put it in the garbage can. Then she reached into the bathtub and retrieved the clothes deposited there. They were damp, so she balled them up and dumped them in the laundry hamper. At least they were only jeans and tee-shirts and not some of her good suits, which required dry cleaning.

"What do you mean?"

"Don't you see? Whoever did this didn't really destroy things," explained Harry. "They didn't break my dishes or throw food all over the walls. They just emptied the boxes I had packed, spread my clothes all over the house and generally messed things up. They didn't really demolish anything."

"That's true," Raven said. "But you don't think it was just a joke, do you?"

"No. It was a warning to lay off, all right."

"Are some of your things missing?"

Harry hadn't noticed. But under the circumstances, she would be surprised if any of her possessions had been stolen. "I don't know. Let's take a look."

They walked through the house, carefully skirting the books, clothes and other objects scattered on the floor. Nothing was gone. Her television, answering machine, stereo and CD player were in the living room; her clock alarm in the bedroom; her microwave and a second radio in the kitchen; her computer in the office behind the kitchen.

They went back to the living room. "Everything's here," Harry said. She removed a couple of paperbacks from the easy chair in the bay window and sat down.

"Would you like me to fix you a drink?" Raven asked.

"No. I'm too tired."

"Coffee, then?"

"I don't want anything. But go ahead and make a pot for yourself."

"I don't want anything, either," Raven said. "I just thought that you might." She slumped down on the floor beside the easy chair and leaned back against Harry's legs. Harry reached down and placed her hand on Raven's head. The fuzz was just long enough to have grown out of the bristly stage. It felt soft as baby's hair. Harry stroked it and felt herself relax. Her eyes closed.

"Come to bed," Raven eventually whispered. She ran her hand up and down Harry's leg.

"The door —"

"Damn! I forgot about that."

Harry perused the Yellow Pages for ads that promised emergency relief for broken locks, and left the same message on several answering machines. She didn't have much hope that anyone would respond. Instinct told her that there was no easy way to reach even a dedicated locksmith on a Sunday evening. She closed the front door and engaged the chain while Raven carried a chair from the kitchen and forced it under the doorknob. Fat lot of good that would do should someone really want to get in, but Harry didn't have the stamina to stay up all night.

She and Raven walked hand and hand into the bedroom. Harry hung the clothes which had been tossed on the bed in the closet, while Raven removed the books and empty cardboard boxes from the bed.

"What do you want me to do with these?" Raven asked, a pile of books in her arms.

"Just put them over there," Harry replied, pointing to a chair by the window.

Once Raven finished picking up the books, they undressed and got into bed. Although Harry was exhausted and wanted to sleep, Raven had other plans.

"I know you're tired," Raven whispered in her ear.

There was tired, and then there was *tired*. Harry woke up. She ran her fingers over Raven's short hair and then kissed her hard. She slid her hands over Raven's shoulders to her breasts, feeling Raven shudder when she stroked them. Desire blossomed. When Harry felt fingers teasing between her thighs, she held on tight, letting her body float in that space between extreme desire and total release.

Raven groaned and came. "I love you so much ..."

Did she love Raven? Did she?

"Stop thinking," Raven told her.

That was easier said than done. Harry's mind always wandered when she was making love. It was part of the floating. At least until she was so close that she had no choice but surrender.

"Come on, Harriet."

Harry floated through her orgasm, and when she came out the other side she felt spineless. She was asleep in seconds.

She dreamed that she was in Manon and Sue's basement family room, but she was alone. She could hear voices from upstairs, strident voices that spoke in riddles. A commercial on the wide-screen television was trumpeting hairspray. She got up and switched it off, but it turned itself back on. An old black-and-white Humphrey Bogart movie was playing. It seemed to be about gangsters. She turned it off again, and a religious service filled the screen. There was praising of the Lord and the singing of hymns, and general enthusiasm about things spiritual. She turned it off, but this time the station didn't change when the TV started again. The preacher began his sermon, which was about sin and damnation, fire and brimstone.

Perhaps she would have better luck in the kitchen. She left the family room, remembering to turn off the light. The TV was still on, but there was nothing she could do about that. It was dark on the stairs, so she grasped the railing. It was metal, iron probably, and frigid to the touch. The cold spread from the palm of her hand up her arm to her heart, which threatened to stop. Luckily, she reached the top of the stairs before that happened.

She rushed from room to room, but the voices eluded her, slipped away just before she reached them. She heard the doorbell ring, but decided not to answer it. This wasn't her house, after all. She went into the kitchen and snared a piece of piping-hot pizza, flinching when cheese melted over her fingers. She was starving. She took a bite of pizza and began to chew. Some damn idiot was leaning on the doorbell. It occurred to her then that she might be the only person left in the house.

She stuffed the rest of the pizza into her mouth, picked up another piece and rushed toward the front door.

"I'm coming, I'm coming!" she shouted. When she opened the door to the entry, the ringing of the doorbell was as loud as a shrieking woman. She dropped the pizza in a puddle full of cigarette butts and covered her ears. "I'm here!"

She was going to go crazy if that noise didn't stop. She flipped the lock and opened the door.

No one was there.

In fact, there was nothing there at all.

Talk about black holes.

"Harriet, wake up."

Harry moaned and turned over.

"It's for you," Raven said.

Harry sat up. Raven was kneeling on the bed, the telephone in her hand. The doorbell, Harry thought as she took the phone from her lover.

"What time is it?"

"I don't know. I was sound asleep."

"I've just had such a dumb dream."

Raven rubbed Harry's back. "It's okay, you're awake now."

"Yes?" Harry mumbled into the receiver. Her mind felt fuzzy.

"Harry, it's Manon. I hope I didn't disturb you."

Manon's voice faded, but when Harry turned her head, the line crackled even worse. "Manon? Are you still there?"

"Yes," Manon replied through the static. "I shouldn't have used my cell phone. Can you come over?"

Harry rubbed her eyes and glanced at the clock radio on her bedside table. It was just past nine-thirty in the evening. "Can't it wait until tomorrow?"

"I would prefer to speak to you now."

Perhaps Manon knew who had killed Julie. Maybe she wanted to confess. Harry knew that she would have to go. "I'll be there."

"I appreciate it, Harry."

Harry was about to reply when the line went dead. What was going on? She switched off the phone and put it on the bedside table.

"I've got to go back to Manon's," she told Raven. "Will you be all right staying here alone?"

"Of course I will."

"Are you sure?"

"Yes. I'll force the chair under the doorknob once you leave. No one will be able to get in without making a lot of noise," Raven replied. "Or I could come with you."

Harry got out of bed and began to dress. "As long as you think you'll be okay here by yourself, it would be better if I went alone. Manon seems to want to talk, and she might not open up with someone else around. I'll drive. If the roads are really bad, I'll stay there overnight, although I would rather be here with you."

Raven hugged her. "Obviously."

Harry hugged Raven back. They went into the hall, and Harry pulled on her boots and her leather jacket.

"Do the safe thing," Raven said.

Harry nodded, gave her a kiss and left the apartment. She went down the stairs, kicking snow off the side of each step. That way there would be less to shovel later. It had grown much colder since morning, and the snow was dry and powdery. Harry walked around the side of the building to the lane, relieved to see that several other cars had left deep tracks in the snow that she would be able to follow.

Harry brushed the snow from the lock, opened the hatchback and took out a long-handled brush. The first foot or so of snow came off easily, but then she had to scrape ice from the windshield and the rear window. This had better be good, she thought when she had managed to clear a large spot on the driver's side of the windshield. Manon had better have something significant to say. She tossed the brush in the back seat and got in.

The car started after five or six tries, which wasn't bad. She was going to miss her old Datsun, but she couldn't very well take it to Key West with her. It was fine for driving around the city and getting back and forth to work, but it was too old to survive the long drive south. She nudged the gas pedal with her toe and nodded her encouragement when the all-weather tires gripped the snow. She steered into the most clearly defined set of tracks and, once she left the lane, headed north on avenue du Parc. As she had expected, there wasn't much traffic. A car sped past, its brights on, and a few buses rumbled by, but she pretty much had the road to herself. Sometimes it was like that after a storm. She decided to take chemin de la Côte-Ste-Catherine, since it cut across the city. Shortly before she reached it, she switched on the radio. Classical music filled the car. Brahms, she thought. The going was slippery, so she got into the right lane and slowed down. She was afraid of black ice, but she didn't encounter any on her way west.

What was she going to do about Raven? Being with her certainly felt good, but where did they go from there? They hadn't discussed the possibility of living together on a long-term basis, partly because Raven was an American who had spent most of her life in the San Francisco Bay area, while Harry had always lived in Canada, mostly in Montreal. Making a commitment would mean drastic changes for one of them. Harry knew that Raven wanted her to move to San Francisco and, during the summer, she had been tempted to stay. She loved the city, with its hills, its pastel buildings and its fantastic social life. But it didn't feel like home.

Raven professed to love her, and sometimes Harry thought she felt the same way. But she wasn't entirely sure. She didn't always understand Raven. There was the newness of their relationship and their difference in age and also of culture, but it was more than that. Harry was unaccustomed to being on the receiving end of such raw emotions, of such unbridled sexuality. Not that there weren't advantages in being involved with someone so passionate, but it could be disconcerting. Harry wondered what would happen when the honeymoon was over. Would Raven wake up one morning and realize that she was with a woman twice her age, a woman who had already gone through menopause, who was thinking more about retirement than what kind of work to do next, who had trouble keeping off weight and who needed a full night's sleep to be at her best?

Harry turned onto a side-street and parked in the driveway, behind Manon's car. She turned off the ignition and sat for a moment, trying to gather her wits about her. Her car cooled swiftly once the heater was off, prompting her to open the door and get out. She walked up the concrete steps and rang the doorbell, bouncing lightly on her toes until she heard footsteps, at first faint, then louder.

Manon opened the door. She looked upset.

"Come in."

Harry closed the door, flipped the lock and followed her into the house.

"Thanks for coming. I really appreciate it."

"It's okay."

"I was in the kitchen," said Manon. "I ordered Chinese food, enough for two. It's just come. Let's eat first, and then we'll talk."

"I have to call Raven," Harry said once they got to the kitchen. The champagne bottles and empty hors d'oeuvre trays had been cleared away, the counters wiped clean. "She was worried about me driving on the snowy roads." Harry wondered whether to tell Manon about the break-in and decided not to mention it yet, if at all. She wanted to find out why Manon had asked her to drop by, and informing her about the intruder would likely distract her from talking about it.

Manon sat down and began opening boxes. "At least someone cares about you. And you know where the phone is," she said, gesturing to the telephone hanging on the wall near the back door.

Harry nearly swooned when the enticing aroma of Chinese food reached her nose. She called Raven and reassured her that she was fine. "I'll be back as soon as I can," she promised.

"Don't worry," Raven said sleepily. "I'm so tired that I probably won't even notice when you get home."

Harry thought that was stretching the truth a bit, but she didn't say anything.

"Miss you." Raven's voice was intimate, reminding Harry of how passionate their recent lovemaking had been.

"Miss you too," Harry whispered, trying not to feel self-conscious. She hung up and turned back toward the kitchen table.

Manon had already filled her plate with a crispy spring roll, egg fried rice, pineapple chicken and Chinese vegetables.

"You're disgusting, mooning over her like a love-sick calf," she commented, tossing the serving spoon into the carton of vegetables.

"Never mind," Harry responded. She swiftly served herself large helpings of food and began to eat.

"Your appetite is good, too," Manon added.

Harry looked up. "And yours isn't?"

Manon wordlessly emptied the carton of pineapple chicken on top of the rice on her plate.

"You're going to gain weight," Harry commented.

"I always put on a few pounds when Sue leaves me because I end up ordering out all the time." Her tone was casual, but Harry knew better. "But don't worry, I'll take it off as soon as she comes back."

Harry didn't think that Sue was going to be in a hurry to reconcile with Manon this time, and Manon likely knew that. "So Sue found out about your affair with Julie the night Julie was killed."

"Yes — I told her," Manon asked. "That was one of the things I wanted to speak to you about tonight."

According to Sue, she had guessed during the basketball game, and Harry had no reason to doubt her interpretation of events or the timing of her discovery about Manon and Julie's affair. Manon had gone on to tell her Saturday night without realizing that she already knew. Or perhaps Manon realized that Sue had somehow found out about her and Julie and decided to jump in with her confession before Sue confronted her. But Harry was more interested in Manon's description of what had happened between her and Sue and Julie the night Julie had been murdered, so she didn't contradict her.

"Why didn't you say something before?"

Manon looked wary. "Because it would have made you suspect her."

"I do anyway."

"*Mais non* — Sue didn't kill her."

"How do you know?"

"I've lived with Sue most of my adult life, and she's incapable of hurting, much less killing someone."

There had been a time when Harry felt the same way about everyone she knew, but after investigating several murders she was now much less confident about assuming that her friends and acquaintances had peaceful intentions. She could imagine the anger Sue Phillips felt when she realized that Manon and Julie were lovers. How intolerable it must have been for her to be around Julie. She had been forced to act normal at Francine and Julie's house for pizza and beer after the game, on the bus trip to the Laurentians, at dinner on Prince-Arthur and later that evening at the bar. Had Sue become increasingly enraged until she could no longer stomach the sight of her rival? Had jealousy driven her to murder?

Manon pushed away her empty plate. "You don't believe me, do you?"

Harry stared at Manon until Manon looked down. "You haven't told me everything, have you?"

"You always answer a question with a question," Manon said with a curt laugh. "That's vintage Hubbley, all right. Sometimes I don't think you've changed a bit since we were at McGill."

"And you always avoid answering a question by trying to change the subject," Harry retorted. "That's vintage Lachance, and it's been the same since I met you and Francine. Now, what is it?"

"Are you going to go straight to the cops if I tell you?"

"Should I?" Harry asked. She realized that she was, as Manon said, answering a question with a question, but she was actually stalling for time to phrase a tactful response to Manon's query. If the information Manon imparted identified Julie's killer, she would have no other choice but to contact Lieutenant-Detective Gagnon. Despite her strong aversion to him, she was not about to obstruct justice. If, however, Manon's testimony just cast more suspicion on someone, she was under no obligation to report anything to the detective.

"Never mind," said Manon. "You've always been a straight shooter, and I'm certain that you'll do what's right. The reason I'm positive Sue didn't kill Julie is that I came across them out on the patio Saturday night, and Julie was very much alive at that point."

Harry stopped eating. "When was this?"

"I don't know exactly," admitted Manon. "Sometime before I asked Raven to dance."

That hadn't been long before Harry had discovered Julie's body. "Why did you go out on the patio?"

"I was hot and the door was open, so I decided to step out for a moment. Wasn't that why you went out? To cool off a little?"

Harry nodded.

"Well, imagine my surprise when I realized that Sue and Julie were already there, huddled under the overhang," Manon continued. "Sue was obviously telling Julie off, and at first they didn't notice me."

"Could you hear what she was saying?"

"No — the music was too loud. But Sue looked as mad as hell. I've only seen that particular expression on her face a couple of times, thank god," answered Manon. "When Sue loses her temper, she sucks the anger deep inside and her voice gets quieter and quieter until she's nearly whispering. You don't want to listen to what she's saying, but you find yourself moving closer anyway. It's sort of hypnotic."

"Anger can be like that sometimes."

"And then, when you're really close, all hell breaks loose and you start wishing you had never been born. Sue has a horrible temper, just horrible." Manon shifted in her chair and leaned her elbows on the table. "And she certainly lost her temper that night. Julie saw me first. She looked annoyed, as if she hadn't wanted Sue's furious monologue to be interrupted. When Sue realized that Julie's attention had shifted, she stopped talking and turned around."

"What happened then?

"Nothing. Sue stalked back into the bar without saying anything else."

"And you stayed outside with Julie," Harry surmised.

Manon nodded.

"What did you talk about?"

"*Rien du tout*. Not a thing. Julie was too pissed off to talk. When I saw the mood she was in, I went back into the bar. I didn't want to spend a lot of time with her, especially now that Sue knew."

The two friends sat in silence for a few minutes.

"I know what you're thinking," Manon finally said.

Harry poked at the cold food on her plate and then put down her fork. "Do you?"

"You're wondering whether I killed her."

Of course she was. "Why did you tell Sue about your affair with Julie on Saturday night? Why not before?"

Manon didn't answer.

"Come on, Manon — you and Julie were lovers for two years. Why did you wait that long to say something to Sue?"

"You didn't know Julie very well, did you?"

About as well as she had wanted to, but that wasn't the point. She wanted to see Julie through Manon's eyes. "What do you mean?"

"Julie was nuts," Manon said bluntly. "I don't mean that she was insane, but emotionally she was all over the map. She could be as loving as an angel and, the next time I would see her, she would turn on me and be as bitchy as anyone I've ever known. I could never be certain which Julie was going to show up for a date."

"That certainly must have kept you on your toes," Harry commented.

"You'd better believe it!"

"I know she could be manipulative."

"She liked to be in control of whatever situation she was in," agreed Manon.

And she hadn't done badly until someone had killed her, Harry mused. "So what did Julie's domineering personality have to do with the timing of your confession to Sue?"

"Whenever Julie thought I wasn't paying enough attention to her, or got paranoid about my taking her for granted or started thinking that maybe I was overly nervous about being sexually involved with my sister's lover, she would threaten to tell Sue," replied Manon.

"How did you respond when she threatened you?"

"How do you think? I didn't want her to realize how scared I was, so most of the time I pretended that she was joking, even though I was nervous as hell that one day she would follow through and actually say something," Manon said. "See, I was afraid Sue would lose her temper and do something stupid, like tell Francine. But you've got to believe that I didn't kill her."

Harry just looked at her.

"Look, I knew that something was going to give," Manon continued. "I wasn't really in love with her anymore. At least not the way I was in the beginning, although I couldn't tell her that. I loved Sue more than anybody else, even though I haven't been faithful. That's always been *the* major deficiency in my character, I suppose. I couldn't figure out how to tell Julie that I wanted out, but, somehow, I think she knew. I tried to act the same, but now when I think back, I realize that I stopped thinking about her all the time. She must have noticed that I wasn't as desperate to see her as I once was."

"How did she react?"

"How do you think? She had an ego the size of a rock star's," Manon said wryly. "She was furious. Heaven forbid anyone should ever lose interest in Julie Beliveau. She tried harder, and for a while it worked. She was a good lover, you know. She liked sex. But I knew it was only a matter of time before someone else found out about us, and I didn't want that to happen."

"So exactly when did you tell Sue?" Harry asked. Something still wasn't clear about Manon's timing.

"Just before we went out to dinner Saturday night."

"What did she say?"

"That was the strange thing, Harry. We were in the bedroom, changing out of the clothes were wore to the Laurentians. Julie was getting pushier every day, so I knew I had to tell Sue before Julie did it herself. I had no idea how to break the news gently, so I just blurted it out. And yet she didn't react at all."

"She must have said something."

"Actually, she did," Manon acknowledged. "She said, 'What a surprise,' and then she went on getting dressed. I figured that she was in shock, that she would lose her temper and tell me off when it finally sunk in."

"Perhaps she already knew."

Manon blinked. "Do you actually think so? But if she did, why didn't she say something?"

"Perhaps you should ask her that question."

"She's not answering my calls," Manon said. "Her sister says that she doesn't want to talk to me."

Harry wasn't surprised. Manon's story was likely true, but it still didn't explain why she had picked the weekend of the teachers' convention to break the news to Sue. "Had Julie given you a deadline?"

"Actually, yes."

"To do what?"

"She wanted me to leave Sue," Manon responded. "She told me that I had until the end of the weekend to make up my mind."

"How charitable of her," Harry commented. And an additional motive for Manon. "Did she say whether she was intending to leave Francine?"

"I don't know," Manon replied. "I asked her that question, but she wouldn't tell me. I think that she didn't want to commit herself before I did. She was like that; if she thought being evasive or secretive would give her an advantage, she wouldn't give a straight answer. She was very stubborn that way."

Harry recalled what Marg had told her about Julie trying to steal her teaching position in Toronto. "Did she tell you that she was looking for a job in Toronto?"

Manon nodded reluctantly.

"Do you think that she was intending to break up with Francine if she did relocate?"

Maybe," Manon conceded. "But, as I told you, she wouldn't say."

"And you didn't put two and two together," Harry said rather sarcastically.

"What do you mean?"

"Are you going to sit there and tell me that Julie didn't ask you to move to Toronto with her?"

"That's exactly what I'm going to sit here and tell you," Manon answered curtly. "It might be hard to believe, but she didn't once even so much as suggest I should pack up my bags and join her on the trek down the 401 to Toronto."

"But then why did she want you to leave Sue?"

"Maybe she was on a power trip," suggested Manon. "Or maybe she was going to ask me later — you know, if I left Sue."

Harry thought that sounded plausible. But would Julie have actually exchanged one Lachance twin for the other? Perhaps. If she had seriously intended to move to Toronto, she could have left the scandal behind.

"Look, all she said was that if I didn't break up with Sue, she would tell her about our affair," said Manon. "I told her if she did that, I would end our relationship immediately. But I don't think she believed me. I was worried that she would jump the gun. That was why I decided to tell Sue myself."

"Do you have any idea why Julie issued such a ultimatum at that particular time?"

Manon shook her head. "No."

"Perhaps she wanted to end her relationship with you anyway," Harry suggested.

"It didn't feel like that to me," said Manon. "As I said, she got all hot and bothered when she thought I wasn't paying attention."

There was that. But Julie had been the type to want her lovers' undivided attention right up until the minute she booted them out the proverbial door. "Do you think she was worried about Francine finding out?"

"I'm sure she was, although she never talked about. But she was very careful."

"I wonder whether Julie was ever in love with Francine," Harry mused aloud.

"People in love with their partners still have affairs with other women," Manon pointed out.

How well Harry knew from personal experience that this was true. But she had come to believe that this feeling was not love, but an echo of love, the memory of a shared emotion, a habit as yet unlearned.

"And so you were afraid that Julie was going to tell Sue before the deadline ran out," she surmised.

"That's right."

"Weren't you afraid that Francine would somehow learn about your affair with Julie?"

"Terrified, actually."

"Do you know if she ever did?"

"I'm positive that she didn't."

"How can you be so sure?"

"Because if she had found out about what was going on, Francine would have killed me," Manon said with great certainty.

The next day, after work, Harry decided to drive directly from school to Francine Lachance's house on boulevard St-Joseph. She telephoned Raven from the teachers' lounge to let her know that she would be a little late getting home. She considered calling Francine before leaving and then thought better of it. She preferred to arrive unannounced, bearing gifts of food, as was traditional when a death occurred. She stopped at a bakery on avenue du Parc and bought a chocolate cheesecake and a loaf of bread, which she asked them to slice. If Francine was alone, Harry would question her. It would be inconvenient if Francine had company, but if other people had dropped by to express their condolences, Harry would pretend that she was just another visitor.

Most of the snow had been removed from the streets. Harry found a parking space in front of Francine's house. The downstairs door was unlocked, so she rang the doorbell and mounted the interior staircase. The door opened as she reached the top.

"Oh, it's you," Isabelle Lachance said with evident displeasure. Albert Dack was hovering behind her, his shiny bald head reflecting the overhead light, his black overcoat draped over his arm.

"I thought I would bring Francine something to eat," Harry said, holding up the plastic shopping bag.

"Isabelle baked and cooked all night long," Albert announced, looking down his nose at Harry's offerings. "Soup, casseroles, bread, cake —"

"And I'm sure Francine really appreciates it," Harry interrupted. Had they just arrived, or were they getting ready to leave? "Since I've finished teaching for the day, I thought I would keep Francine company for a while. I'd like to see how she's doing and give her this cheesecake and loaf of bread."

"Francine's been through a shock. She needs her rest," grumbled Isabelle.

Albert gave a slight nod of agreement.

"You know, we never finished the conversation we were having during the brunch at Manon and Sue's yesterday," Harry said, keeping her voice pleasant. "What was Julie holding over you, anyway?"

"I don't know what you're talking about," Isabelle answered, her tone haughty.

"It had something to do with why you suddenly switched from physical education to primary teaching methods, didn't it?" Harry ventured.

Isabelle's face crumbled.

Albert rushed past her and propelled his body between Harry and his wife, as if to protect her from Harry's verbal assault. "How dare you insinuate —"

"No, Albert, she's right," Isabelle interjected.

Albert stood indecisively between them. With his dangling arms and his tall, bony frame, he looked more like an adolescent than a middle-aged man.

"Give it up, Albert," Harry urged. "Someone will eventually find out anyway, and it's better that it be me than a member of the police force."

Albert bit his lip and withdrew. "How that bitch ever found out, I'll never know," he muttered in French as he rushed down the stairs. Moments later, the door slammed behind him.

"He can't deal with it — he always runs away," Isabelle murmured.

Harry knew then what their secret was and why Albert followed his wife everywhere, afraid to let her out of his sight, especially when she visited her lesbian sisters.

"You fell in love with a woman when you were studying at McGill, didn't you?"

Isabelle made an effort to compose herself. "I wouldn't exactly put it like that," she remarked. "Suffice it to say that there were a lot of lesbians in the physical-education department, which is certainly not news to you. And one of them was attracted to me. *Very* attracted to me.

She made a total fool of herself. She followed me everywhere and repeatedly asked me out, but of course I refused. I was already engaged to Albert then."

"If that was the case, why did you stop studying physical education?" Harry asked.

Isabelle had pulled herself together. She opened the closet door and took her winter coat from the hanger. "I had second thoughts about a career in that field."

"Why?"

"What, is it against the law for a woman to change her mind?"

"You make it sound so innocent."

"Well, that's what it was."

"It couldn't possibly have had anything to do with Albert, could it?"

"What are you talking about?"

"I'll bet he didn't like you hanging around with so many lesbians," Harry said. "He probably pestered you to change to another faculty."

"So what?"

"Why didn't Albert trust you, Isabelle? Was it simply because he was suspicious by nature or prejudiced about things he didn't understand, or did you perhaps respond just a little bit to your female admirer? Did you give her some encouragement? After all, your older sisters were both lesbians. The lifestyle wasn't entirely new to you."

Isabelle looked cross. "Albert's not homophobic."

Harry didn't believe her. "Well, what, then?"

"Oh, all right. So I did play along with her a little," Isabelle admitted reluctantly. "I probably shouldn't have, but I was young and impressionable then. And it was quite flattering to have someone act so crazy about me. What harm was there in it, after all?"

Quite a lot, Harry reflected. She had never been jerked around by a slumming straight woman, but she knew plenty of lesbians who had been, and the results were invariably unpleasant to observe.

"Did you sleep with her?"

Isabelle was affronted. She wrapped her scarf around her neck and put her coat on. "You don't expect me to answer that question, do you?"

"Not if you would rather tell the police instead," Harry responded with a casual shrug.

It didn't take Isabelle long to resolve that particular conundrum. "No, I didn't *sleep* with her."

"As in having sex," Harry clarified.

"I understood what you meant."

"But you did fool around a little," surmised Harry.

"I didn't do anything wrong," Isabelle protested. "She was insistent, that's all."

"And you were curious."

"Well, yes."

"What happened? Did you freak out when you realized that you enjoyed fooling around, that you were more like your sisters than you ever imagined?"

Isabelle capitulated. "I was shocked. I never thought I would feel attracted to a woman. Hell, I could see what people thought about homosexuals, how they made jokes about diesel dykes and limp-wristed faggots, and discriminated against gay people, and I didn't *want* to be like Manon and Francine. So I broke up with her before it went too far. But it was hard seeing her in class every day. And you were right; Albert was threatened. That was why I switched from physical education to primary teaching methods."

"Did Albert find out about your attraction to her?"

Isabelle glanced down the stairs, but the front door was still closed. "No, he didn't. How could he? I never told him. He just thought that I got tired of her having a crush on me. I also told him that I found all the physical training difficult and was no longer certain I wanted to work in that field. Frankly, I think he was relieved when I got out of there. He still doesn't know what really happened."

"How on earth did Julie find out? Was your girlfriend someone Julie knew? Someone any of us would have known?"

Isabelle pulled a pair of gloves from her pocket and put them on. "No. And don't call her my 'girlfriend,' because she wasn't. She dropped out of school after one term, and I never saw her again. Don't forget that you were all seniors when I started university, and you didn't pay much attention to lowly first-year students. I've often wondered how Julie found out. Someone must have told her, but she never mentioned who it was."

"What did Julie want from you?"

"Nothing, really."

Harry was incredulous. Women like Julie always wanted something. "Are you certain? Why did she tell you that she knew about it, then?"

"Because she was a horrible person. Isn't that reason enough?" Isabelle retorted, her anger finally breaking through. "I could never understand why my sister got involved with her. She tried to poison Francine's relationship with the rest of the family by telling her that we were up to no good, that we were plotting against her or attempting to exclude her from family events. Francine took it with a grain of salt, but when we confronted her with Julie's lies, she just brushed us off by saying that Julie had a suspicious nature and was just trying to protect her. Protect her from what, I ask you? We've always been a close-knit family, and Julie was jealous."

"Did Julie ask for money or some other compensation to keep quiet about what happened when you were in university?"

Isabelle buttoned her coat and raised its fur collar around her neck. "She told me that she knew, but she didn't threaten me or ask me for anything."

Harry didn't believe her. "That doesn't sound like Julie."

"Perhaps not, but it's the truth," Isabelle professed. "I think she got off on the thought that she could ruin my life with a word to Albert, or to my vice-principal, for that matter. She also knew that there wasn't a damn thing I could do to stop her from holding it over my head forever."

Except kill her, Harry reflected. But she said nothing to Isabelle.

"Anyway, I had better go. Albert is waiting for me in the car, and he's not the most patient man in the world."

Harry watched Isabelle rush down the staircase and leave the building without a backward glance. Fear that a twenty-five-year-old affair with another woman would expose her to both personal and professional censure certainly constituted a strong motive for murder. And what about Albert? Had he somehow discovered that his wife had been sexually involved with a woman and that Julie knew? Would he have tried to protect her from the possibility of professional ruin by murdering Julie? Could either of them have left the café and rushed across the street to the bar to confront, and then kill, Julie without anyone in their entourage noticing that they were gone for an overly long time? If so, they would have had to arrange a specific time to meet with Julie. Either of them could have ransacked the apartment and written the warning on the bathroom mirror, although the cold-blooded way in which it had been done pointed more to Albert than to Isabelle.

"Did my baby sister leave?" Francine Lachance asked.

Harry jumped. "You startled me," she said, laughing unsteadily.

Francine materialized from the shadows. The sun had set while Harry and Isabelle stood talking in the foyer, and there were no lights on in the hall. "That seems to be a habit of mine," Francine said, her voice flat. "I woke up a few minutes ago."

"Isabelle and Albert just left. And I brought you a little something," Harry said, holding her plastic bag out in front of her.

"You and half the rest of the world," Francine said. She took the bag from Harry, turned around and walked toward the dining room.

Harry kicked off her boots and tagged along, wondering whether Francine had expected her to leave once her contribution had been delivered.

"Isabelle said she brought you quite a bit of food," she remarked once they reached the kitchen.

Francine spun around and looked at Harry, apparently surprised to see that she was still there.

"Yes," she agreed, although she clearly wasn't interested. "Help yourself to something to eat," she added. "I'll never get through all this, and Isabelle wouldn't take anything."

The counter was partially covered with casseroles, some of them topped with glass covers, others awash in foil or plastic wrap. On the kitchen table were several plates of cookies, loaves of bread, pies and cakes.

"Isabelle and Albert brought all this?" Harry asked.

"Some of it. The rest came from friends and neighbours." Francine removed the contents from Harry's bag. "This is the first cheesecake, though. Want some?"

"Sure." Harry loved chocolate cheesecake, but she never bought it for herself. It was too fattening.

Francine took two plates from the kitchen cabinet and two forks and a knife from one of the drawers. She cut two large pieces of chocolate cheesecake, manoeuvred them onto the plates and handed one to

Harry. "Coffee would go good with this, but Isabelle and Albert drank the whole pot. Do you want to wait while I make another?"

"No," Harry said immediately, and then added, "not unless you do."

"It doesn't matter," Francine responded. As soon as she sat down, they both picked up their forks and ate wordlessly until their plates were clean.

Harry sat back in her chair, overwhelmed by the lethargic feeling that descended when she had consumed a large quantity of sugar. Francine soon interrupted her reverie.

"What did you want to see me about?"

Harry didn't know quite where to begin.

"You didn't drop by just to give me a chocolate cheesecake and a loaf of bread, did you?"

Harry knew it would do no good to lie. "Not really."

"I've heard you've been asking a fair number of embarrassing questions."

Harry gave her an inquisitive look and wondered whether Francine had been the person who had broken into her flat and used Raven's lipstick to write that message on her bathroom mirror. If so, Francine was certainly toying with her now.

"So do you still think I killed Julie?"

"I don't know. Did you?"

Francine gave her a smile. "No."

Well, that made it unanimous. Evidently, no one had killed Julie Beliveau. Perhaps she had hit herself with a brick for the hell of it and thereby inadvertently inflicted a fatal injury.

"You're an extremely jealous woman."

"So what?"

"Jealousy can be a very strong motive for violent behaviour."

"Oh, come on," scoffed Francine. "Can't you do any better than that?" She got up, opened the fridge, removed a carton of milk and put it on the table. She took two glasses from the cabinet over the sink and filled them with milk. "Here."

Harry felt like she was being alternately disarmed and intimidated, which left her slightly off balance.

"Of course I was jealous about Manon and Julie. It would be stupid to deny it."

Harry nearly choked. Milk spilled over the side of her glass. She lowered it and set it on the table beside her empty plate. "You knew about their relationship?"

"Tell me this: Could you live with someone and not sense that something had changed?"

Apparently so, Harry thought sadly, because that was precisely what had happened with Judy. "No," she fibbed.

"That's it, then," Francine said with a self-satisfied nod. "As I told you before, I really loved Julie, but that didn't mean that I wasn't aware of her faults. She was one of the worst flirts on earth, and I knew damn well that it was only a matter of time before somebody took her up on it."

"But you certainly couldn't have imagined that the someone would be your twin sister," said Harry.

"Touché," Francine said softly.

"Sorry."

"I know you didn't mean to rub it in," Francine conceded. "But if you look at it logically, something like that was bound to happen. People think that Manon and I aren't much alike, but they're wrong. We're quite similar in our likes and dislikes and in our emotional responses, not to mention our taste in women. It's just that Manon went to university and I dropped out of high school, so she's a lot better educated than me. But Manon was attracted to Julie for the same reasons I was, and Julie was attracted to Manon because she's a lot like me."

That was all well and fine and logical, except that Harry doubted that most twins raided their siblings' beds. "When did you realize that Julie and Manon had become lovers?"

"Right from the time they got together," Francine said. "Listen, do you want another piece of cheesecake?"

"No, thanks," Harry responded, although her mouth filled with saliva at the idea. "Weren't you upset when you found out?"

Francine made a face at her. "I never said I wasn't upset," she said impatiently. "Wouldn't you be?"

"I'm a little confused, here," Harry admitted. "If their affair bothered you, why didn't you do something about it?"

"Don't you think I wanted to? But I was afraid I would lose Julie if I came down hard on her."

"And Manon?"

"What about her?" Francine's tone was harsh. She rose abruptly from the table and turned her back on Harry.

"Did you think you would lose her too?"

"You think you're smart, Hubbley, but you don't know what you're talking about," Francine retorted angrily. She wheeled around and faced Harry. "Manon is my *sister*, my *twin sister*. If I had said one word to her about what she was doing with Julie, if I had mentioned that she was hurting me even a little, she would have stopped seeing Julie *just like that*. No second thoughts, no arguments, no regrets. She would have broken it off in a minute."

"But you never said that one word."

"No, I didn't."

"Why not?"

Francine's anger diminished as swiftly as it had risen. "Does it matter now?"

"Perhaps."

"I thought they would tire of each other before long," Francine said. "But that's not the way it happened. Oh, things cooled off a little after a while, and toward the end I think they were having problems, but it lasted a lot longer than I imagined it would."

"Until Julie died."

Francine stared at Harry, a hard, impenetrable look on her face. "Yeah. Until she died."

The phone rang.

Francine answered it on the third ring and then handed the receiver to Harry. It was only when she said "Hello" that Harry realized how dry her mouth was.

"It's me," Raven said. "The locksmith has been and gone, and you are now the proud owner of a deadbolt lock and a doorframe reinforced with a metal strip which also has some insulation attached to it. Dual purpose — keep the crooks out and the heat in. But that's not why I called. Lieutenant-Detective Gagnon is here to see you."

"Dammit," Harry murmured. "Can you keep him entertained until I get there?"

"No problem," Raven said blithely. "See, I didn't let him in."

"What?"

"I told him my mother taught me never to let strange men in the house when I was home alone."

Harry burst out laughing. "I'll be there soon."

"*Ciao*, then."

"*Ciao*." Harry got up and replaced the receiver in its cradle. "I've got to go," she said to Francine, who looked as though she didn't care whether Harry stayed or went.

"Thanks for the cheesecake."

"It's the least I could do."

"You don't believe me, do you?"

"I don't know what to believe."

Francine raised her head and gave Harry a curt nod of acknowledgement.

"I'll be in touch," Harry added.

"I'm sure you will."

Harry was grateful that Francine didn't accompany her to the front door. She dressed swiftly, tugged on her boots and hurried down the stairs. A parking ticket was stuck under her left windshield wiper; she had forgotten that there was no parking on this side of the street after four o'clock in the afternoon. She removed it from the windshield and tucked it in the pocket of her leather jacket. Her Datsun started on the second try. The weather had moderated and it was no longer cold. The sun had come out around noon, and the snow was slowly melting. It would freeze again overnight, of course.

Harry flicked her turn signal, checked her side mirror and pulled out into traffic. She wasn't looking forward to dealing with Lieutenant-Detective Gagnon, but other than barricading herself inside her apartment with Raven and leaving him sitting in his car outside on the street, there wasn't much other choice. Of course she could keep on driving south until she reached the Champlain Bridge, which crossed the St Lawrence River, take the Eastern Townships Autoroute and head down to the Quebec-Vermont border, and *voilà*: Three or four days from now, she would be in Key West.

Instead, she drove around the block until she hit l'Esplanade, turned into the laneway and parked behind her apartment building. She might be a lot of things, but never let it be said that she was a quitter.

Lieutenant-Detective Gagnon was mightily displeased. He was irritated that Harry hadn't immediately been available when he wanted to talk to her. He was resentful that not only had Raven refused to let him wait inside their apartment, she had also been within her rights to refuse him entry. And he was churlish that the heater in his car wasn't working well, with the result that his feet were like blocks of ice by the time Harry sauntered around the side of her building and began to climb the stairs to her second-floor flat.

"Madame Hubbley!" the detective called.

Harry stopped and turned around. "Yes?"

"You certainly took your time getting here."

Harry didn't reply. She wondered whether she had to answer his questions, then decided that she might as well. If she didn't, he was capable of hounding her, of approaching her at school and generally making her life miserable. During the brunch yesterday, he had threatened that she would be high on his shit list, and now here he was, breathing down her neck.

When they reached the top of the stairs, Harry turned and looked at the detective. "I want you to tell you something before we go in," she said. "I don't plan to put up with any rough stuff. I expect you to act professionally; otherwise, I won't answer your questions. Do you understand?"

Harry would have preferred a verbal response to his abrupt nod, but she didn't push her luck. She rang the doorbell and waited for Raven to open the door. As she led the detective into her apartment, the tantalizing odour of good cooking wafted from the kitchen.

Raven gave Harry a kiss on the cheek. "Don't take too long. Dinner will be ready soon."

Raven returned to the kitchen without so much as a glance in the detective's direction. Gagnon seemed to be ignoring her too, which was just as well.

"Let's go in the living room," she said.

Harry turned the wing chair around and sat in it. The detective unbuttoned his winter coat, removed a half-full cardboard carton from a wood chair and perched on the edge of it. He withdrew a ballpoint pen and his tattered notebook from the inside pocket of his suit jacket and took his time leafing through it.

"Do you still claim that you weren't having an affair with the deceased?" he finally asked.

"Of course I wasn't," Harry responded impatiently. "I told you yesterday that she was just flirting with me, and that anyone who knew her could confirm that she treated everyone that way at one time or another."

He made a note. "I've heard that."

"Then why keep asking me?"

"Because it's my job," he said is a surprisingly mild voice. "Look, I don't really think you killed her, but I have to cover all the bases. What if you saw something that might lead me to the perpetrator, something you're not aware has any significance because you can't see the big picture? That's why I have to ask you a lot of questions, whether you're a suspect or not."

Harry reluctantly conceded the point.

"Only that seems to be what you've been doing, too," he added casually.

She had let her guard slip, but it immediately snapped back into place. There was probably no point in evasion, but the urge to hide — or at least minimize — what she had been up to was overwhelming. "I don't know what you mean."

"An interesting report appeared on my desk this morning," Gagnon said. "It was about a break and enter at this exact address, and it just happened to mention that there was a warning written with lipstick on your bathroom mirror."

"Oh, that," Harry said, sounding disdainful.

A smile momentarily curved Gagnon's lips. "Precisely. It occurred to me to wonder what might have motivated someone to leave you that specific message. Have you been snooping, Madame Hubbley?"

Harry didn't particularly like his choice of words, but she wasn't about to be provoked. If the detective found out how many people she had interrogated and the large number of questions she had asked them, she would be in deep trouble. Not only would he read her the riot act, he would likely never leave her alone again.

"No more than the next person," she replied.

He looked sceptical. "Why would someone bother to break in here and write 'Stop asking questions' on your mirror, then?"

"I have no idea."

The detective pursed his lips. "The investigating officers noted that you weren't sure if anything was taken during the burglary, so they left you a report form to fill out. Was anything missing?"

"No."

"So the main reason for the break-in must have been to write the message on your mirror."

"It was probably just a joke," Harry said with a shrug.

"I doubt it. It looks to me as if someone was warning you off."

Harry forced herself to laugh. "That's ludicrous. I haven't done anything."

The detective studied her for a moment, then closed his notebook and returned it and the pen to the inside pocket of his jacket. "You're playing a dangerous game, Madame Hubbley. Someone who has killed once will kill again if you ask too many questions or if you get in the way or get too close to the truth. I would take the warning seriously, if I were you. I can't spare a man to watch your house or follow you around to make sure you don't get into trouble or no one comes after you, so be careful."

"Don't worry," Harry said with more bravado than she felt.

Lieutenant-Detective Gagnon stood up, a defeated look on his face. "I can't make it any plainer than that. Just don't get in my way," he added as he buttoned up his winter coat. "And if you do find out anything of importance, you had better make sure I hear about it ten seconds later."

Harry nodded, then realized that she had just admitted her guilt.

"I can see myself out," he said, a mulish look on his face.

Damn him, Harry thought. She waited until she heard the front door close and then got up, went into the hall and turned the key in the lock. She switched off the living-room light and went into the kitchen, her stomach growling with hunger despite the large piece of cheesecake she had gobbled up at Francine's.

"What did he want?" Raven asked. She poked a fork into a pot and removed several Chinese noodles, nibbling on one to test whether it was done.

"The usual," Harry replied, looking at the stir-fry cooking on the stove. It smelled of a mix of spices, and contained sliced onion; mushrooms; red, green and yellow peppers; sliced celery; chopped chestnuts and large cubes of tofu. "This looks great."

"I went shopping after the locksmith was finished," Raven said as she returned the Chinese noodles to the pot. "They need to cook for a few minutes longer."

Harry put her arms around Raven and kissed the back of her neck. She smelled of soap and spices.

"There wasn't a thing in this house I could use to make a decent meal," Raven said. "Is your fridge always empty?" She turned around and buried her face in Harry's shoulder.

"I've been busy," Harry answered. The truth was, she didn't cook much when she was alone, although she had been the main preparer of meals when she and Judy had lived together. But it wasn't much fun to cook for one. There were always too many leftovers, and, besides, she found she spent longer making dinner than consuming it. Somehow, she was not a success as a single person in the culinary department.

"Don't evade the question," Raven whispered in her ear as she toyed with Harry's buttocks. "Don't you like cooking?"

"Of course I do," Harry responded, somewhat distracted by what Raven's hand was doing. "I've just never been fond of eating alone."

"So you don't bother eat to at all," Raven surmised. "Or you eat all your meals standing up, or while reading a newspaper or watching TV."

Harry laughed. She began kissing Raven's cheek, then moved to her lips. They kissed for a long time before Raven broke away.

"The noodles are going to be soft," Raven said.

Harry felt a fierce sexual hunger, which must have been written all over her face because Raven turned off the stove and moved the noodles and stir-fry from the burners.

"Soggy noodles aren't the end of the world," she said, reaching out for Harry.

Their kiss became increasingly urgent. "We should move into the bedroom," Harry murmured as Raven's hands moved under her sweater and undid the clasp on her bra.

"Later," Raven muttered, reaching forward to cup Harry's breasts.

"No, now," Harry insisted. Her knees felt weak, and she didn't relish the idea of making love on the kitchen floor.

Raven released her, but instead of heading toward the bedroom, she sat on a chair and pulled Harry down until she was straddling her.

"What are you doing?" Harry sputtered when Raven shoved her sweater up over her breasts and unzipped her pants.

"Making love to you."

Harry had never done it sitting up on a chair in the kitchen, but she supposed there was a first time for everything. She put her arms around Raven and let Raven stroke her body until she trembled with desire. She grasped Raven's hand and forced it down between her thighs and then rocked back and forth until she came, a wild, wonderful orgasm which left her breathless and sweaty.

Then the doorbell rang.

Raven stirred. "Shit."

"We won't answer it," Harry whispered. She began to touch Raven's breasts through her sweatshirt, but Raven held her off.

The doorbell rang again.

"It might be important," Raven reminded her. "Maybe it's about the murder."

"Dammit," Harry muttered plaintively. She got up, closed her pants and hurried toward the front door. She pulled her bra down and lowered her sweater. She was uncomfortable with her bra half on and half off, but she didn't have time to stop and redo the hooks.

"I'm coming," she shouted when the doorbell sounded again. She switched on the hall light and looked through the peephole. It was Sue Phillips. Elizabeth Martin and Sophie Lister were standing behind her. Harry opened the door.

"Are we interrupting something?" Sue asked. She had a large suitcase in her hand, and Liz was carrying a small one.

Did it look that obvious? Harry ran her hand through her hair and realized how mussed it was.

"No, not really," she lied.

An uncomfortable silence arose among the four of them, but it was mercifully short.

"You may wonder why I've got this with me," Sue said, gesturing to her suitcase with her free hand. "Well, it didn't work out at my sister's. She already had company, and what with her husband and the kids, the house was too crowded. I ended up sleeping on the living-room sofa, which is way outside my comfort zone, especially in a straight household. You did say that I could stay here, so I thought I would take you up on your offer."

"Of course," Harry said at once, trying to inject some enthusiasm into her voice. "Come in, come in." She stood aside to let them into the apartment, then closed the front door. "We were just about to have dinner. I don't know whether there's enough for five, but we can always make more."

"I've already eaten," Sue remarked.

"And Sophie and I are going out to dinner," Liz announced.

"Sue asked us to drop her off first," added Sophie, giving Liz an affectionate glance.

Harry wondered whether Liz and Sophie were going out on a date or whether they had simply come together in aid of Sue. Harry had thought that Sophie and Marg Alexander were interested in each other, but she could have been wrong. Sophie was from Quebec City and Liz lived in Montreal, both were single, and the two cities weren't all that far apart. Marg Alexander was single, too. But for a francophone, Toronto was a lot farther from Quebec City than from Montreal, psychologically if not geographically. Perhaps the enigmatic, dark-eyed Sophie, whom none of them had known before she had been chosen at random to round out their pick-up basketball team Friday night, was simply playing the field.

"Manon's got the car," Sue explained.

Liz studied her watch. "We had better be off or we'll be late for our reservation."

"*Au revoir*. And thanks for the lift," Sue said.

There were desultory hugs and kisses, and then Sophie and Liz left. Harry locked the door and turned to Sue. "I'll take your coat," she said, fussing around her.

"I know where the closet is," Sue said somewhat irascibly.

Harry backed off, wary of Sue's quick temper.

"I'm sorry," Sue said with a sigh. "But you don't have to baby me. I've been through this more times than you'll ever know and I always land on my feet. So just show me to my room and I'll get out of your way."

But it was more complicated than that. Harry hadn't been expecting company, so the trundle bed in her office had to be extricated from under a pile of boxes. Then Harry had to find sheets, pillows, pillowcases and blankets as well as towels and a facecloth, which under ordinary circumstances wouldn't have been difficult. But her mind was muddled from recent lovemaking and much of her extra linen was already packed, so by the time everything was organized, the Chinese noodles were nearly too mushy to eat and the stir-fry had to be reheated, making the vegetables soft rather than crisp.

It was nearly eight o'clock when Harry and Raven finally sat down at the kitchen table.

"I did my best," Raven apologized after she scooped an ample helping of Chinese noodles and tofu stir-fry onto Harry's plate. "At least the bread isn't overcooked," she added, referring to the multigrain loaf she had purchased at a local bakery.

"Everything looks delicious," Harry protested.

"If you like baby food."

Harry sampled dinner. "It tastes good, anyway."

"You would never make it as a food critic."

Harry smiled at her and they ate in companionable silence. How would she define the ability to feel both incredible passion and quiet comfort in the presence of a woman? Was that love? What about the capacity to feel good, to relax and not wonder about protecting her back?

"What are you thinking about?" Raven asked.

Harry reached for a piece of bread and began buttering it. "Love. And you."

"I won't interrupt, then."

Did she care enough about Raven to want to live with her? Should she invite her to move to Key West? What if Raven didn't want to live there? For all of its sophisticated veneer and the visibility of gay men and lesbians, Key West was still part of conservative, red-neck Florida. What if Raven rejected Key West and asked Harry to come back to San Francisco with her? What would Harry do then? Would they be stalemated again, their relationship relegated to phone calls and frequent visits between opposite coasts of the United States?

"Would you like some coffee?" asked Raven. "It's decaffeinated."

So Raven had replenished her supply of coffee too. "That would be nice."

"Shall I ask Sue if she wants some?"

"She might already be asleep. I wonder if her door is closed."

"Let me check." Raven got up and walked down the hall. She returned a minute later. "She doesn't want coffee, but she wouldn't mind having a key to the front door."

"No problem," Harry said, and then she realized that the lock had been changed today. "Wait — how many keys did you ask the locksmith for?"

Raven opened the freezer and took out a tin of coffee. "Just two. They were quite expensive."

"I guess we'll have to give her one," Harry said. "Does she need it tonight, or can she wait until tomorrow? I'm sure the locksmith can make another one."

"I asked her that question, and she said she would prefer to have it tonight." Raven filled the pot with water from the tap, measured enough coffee for four cups and plugged in the pot.

Harry glanced at her watch. It was nearly eleven. "What on earth for?"

"She said she might go out later."

That was altogether too curious for Harry.

"I wonder where?"

Raven looked at her. "She didn't say."

"I suppose I could give her my key."

"I left it on top of the bedroom dresser for you," Raven said. "Go ahead and give it to her. I'll clean up, even though it's your turn."

"Thanks." How easily they had reverted to the routines they had established when she had lived with Raven in San Francisco. If Raven cooked, Harry washed dishes. If Raven vacuumed, Harry dusted. If Raven shopped, Harry put everything away. This equitable division of labour worked well; for one thing, it prevented the development of petty grievances and, for another, it made it easier for Harry to feel that she had some ownership of Raven's home. Harry supposed that the same routine was serving the same purposes for Raven now that she was in Montreal.

Harry walked into the bedroom and retrieved her new key from the dresser. She went to her office and rapped on the door.

"Come in," called Sue.

Harry opened the door and went inside. Sue was sitting in her desk chair, reading a magazine she had taken from a box. It was an old copy of *Ms*.

"Here's your key," Harry said. "It's a deadbolt, so you have to lock the door from the inside and the outside."

"Thanks." Sue took the key from Harry and slipped it in the pocket of her jeans. "I'm familiar with them. We have one too."

Harry hovered, even though Sue had once again bent her head over the magazine.

"Did you want something?" Sue finally asked.

Only her long-deceased grandmother had been able to make Harry feel like an intruder in her own house. "Are you planning to go out tonight?"

Sue gave her a what's-it-to-you look. "Maybe. Why, is that a problem?"

"No," Harry replied evenly.

"I probably won't, but I don't like feeling that I can't," Sue added.

And that would have to do, Harry realized. "I'll see you tomorrow, then."

"Goodnight, Harry. And thanks."

Where was she planning to go? Harry was burning with curiosity. But when she returned to the kitchen, she soon discovered that Raven was burning with something else entirely. Before long, Harry forgot about Sue. She and Raven abandoned their coffee and retired to the bedroom, where they brought some unfinished business to a most satisfactory conclusion.

Tuesdays were Harry's worst days. She had no spare periods, and, to further exacerbate matters, she had a double class with the Secondary One girls, who, she had learned through painful experience over the years, were the worst malingerers and complainers. By lunchtime, she was exhausted and ready for a shower, which she had no opportunity to take because she was on cafeteria duty this week.

She and Raven had overslept and there had been no time to prepare lunch, so toward the end of lunch hour, once the majority of students had passed through the line in the cafeteria, Harry bought a bowl of soup, a small salad and a coffee. She had just sat down at an empty table when one of her students approached.

"Ms. Hubbley, there's a lady waiting for you outside," the Secondary Four student said.

Harry was starving. "Tell her I'll be there in a few minutes." She began to spoon soup into her mouth, but the student lingered. "What it is, Crystal?"

"She said it was urgent."

"I'll tell you what: Ask her to wait in the teachers' lounge," Harry suggested.

"I don't think she's going to want to," the student said, her voice taking on a note of hesitancy.

Harry stopped eating and glanced up at Crystal. Her cropped, jet-black hair made her creamy skin look sickly pale, an effect which was accentuated by lipstick so red it was nearly neon. She could have been Raven's younger sister.

"What do you mean?"

"She looks like somebody beat her up," Crystal said.

Harry's spoon clattered to her tray. Had someone broken into the house again and attacked Raven? "What did she say her name was?"

"She didn't."

"Where is she?"

"Just inside the front door," replied Crystal.

Harry got up and started for the exit, her lunch and her duties as a monitor forgotten.

"I'll put your tray away, Ms. Hubbley," Crystal called after her, but Harry didn't hear her.

She wanted to run, but she didn't want to alarm the students loitering in the halls. The paltry amount of soup and salad she had consumed churned in her practically empty stomach when she thought of Raven being hurt. She should have paid attention to the warning on her mirror and listened to what Lieutenant-Detective Gagnon said. But it wasn't Raven who was standing inside the front door of the school, her face partially wrapped is a long, woollen scarf; it was Manon Lachance.

"What's wrong?" Harry hissed, grasping her by the arm.

Manon looked around warily and then dropped the scarf. She had a black eye and there was a large bruise on her cheek.

"Good god!"

"It's not a pretty sight, is it?"

"Let me get my coat and we'll go have coffee," Harry said, recovering her equilibrium. "There's a café around the corner."

"Don't you have to work?"

"I'll go to office and explain that I've suddenly become ill," Harry said. "Students do it all the time."

"Much more convincingly than teachers, of course." Manon grinned and then winced. "Dammit, that hurts."

"Wait here a minute," Harry said.

She rushed to the office and made her excuses. Yes, it would be inconvenient, but she couldn't help it. She was sick. She had developed a sudden fever. Someone else would have to take her afternoon sessions. She was quite firm about it; friendship overrode duty in this instance. She retrieved her winter coat from the teachers' lounge and returned to the front door.

"Let's go."

The lunchtime crowd had thinned out by the time they reached the Zorba Café. Despite its Greek name, it served greasy fast foods which high-school students with a little extra cash in their pockets found infinitely more appetizing than the bland fare served in the school cafeteria. Harry led Manon to a booth in the back. They piled their winter coats on the wood bench and sat down beside them. Manon kept her scarf wrapped around her neck, but it didn't hide her black eye or the bruise under it.

"*Bon*. So what will you gals have?" the waitress asked in French, studiously ignoring Manon's battered face.

Harry was famished. She ordered a cheeseburger with fries and a chocolate milkshake. Manon asked for a coffee.

"Are you sure that's all you want?" asked Harry.

"If I eat anything, I'll be sick."

The waitress abruptly left.

"I guess she doesn't want that," Manon said wryly.

"Who did that to you?" Harry asked, switching to English. "And don't tell me you ran into a doorknob or fell down the stairs."

Manon waited until the waitress had served her coffee before she answered Harry's question. "Somebody broke into my house last night. I woke up and heard the person walking around. The lights didn't work, so I took the flashlight I keep in the drawer of my bedside table and went looking for whoever it was."

Harry sat up straight. Perhaps the same person had broken into her flat and Manon's house! "That was foolish of you! You're supposed to call the police if you think someone is breaking in."

"Don't you think I know that? But I was mad as hell, and all I could think of was to catch the bugger."

"So what happened?"

Manon gingerly touched the bruise on her face. "I found whoever it was, or perhaps it would be more correct to say that she found me."

Harry sat back and let the waitress serve her burger, fries and milkshake.

"Anything else?" the waitress asked. She plunked a bottle of ketchup on the table.

"I'd like a refill," Manon said.

The waitress sighed. "I'll be back in a minute."

"She didn't have to take it personally," Manon remarked.

It was typical of Manon to turn everything into a joke when she was upset. Harry up-ended the ketchup over her plate and slapped the bottom of the bottle. Ketchup spewed from it and covered several French fries. "That's what always happens to me," Harry griped. She picked up her burger and took a big bite. "So what did you do?"

"I went downstairs, flashlight in hand but not turned on," Manon said. "I could hear the intruder in the kitchen, so I walked in that direction. I must have spooked her, because before I knew it, the door bounced open and she ran right into me. Her arms were up, and one of her elbows connected with my face. Then she was gone."

Harry took another bite of her burger. It was satisfyingly greasy, the roll coated with mayo and ketchup and stuffed with a thick slices of tomato and dill pickle and several pieces of iceberg lettuce. "So it was a woman?"

Manon nodded as the waitress refilled her coffee cup.

"How do you know?"

Manon poured milk into her cup, added two sugar cubes and stirred. "You know who it was, don't you?"

Manon covered her face with her hands. "It was Sue."

Harry put her burger on her plate. "Are you certain?"

"Don't you think I would know?"

"Did she said something when you ran into each other?"

"Not a word."

"So you turned on your flashlight and you actually saw her, then."

"The flashlight got knocked out of my hand when she ran into me. It rolled into a corner."

Harry took a drink of her milkshake and speared several French fries on her fork. They were so drenched with ketchup that they were soggy. "If you didn't see her and she didn't make any noise, how do you know it was Sue?"

"I could smell her shampoo," Manon replied. "I gave her a bottle of *Fleur d'esprit* in her stocking last year for Christmas, and she really liked it. She bought some more when that ran out, and now she uses it all the time."

"And that's the only way you could tell who it was?"

"Isn't that enough?"

"Maybe. But that's a pretty popular shampoo, and a lot of other people use it," Harry said. "Besides, why would Sue break into your house when she could have used her key?"

"At three in the morning?"

"Why not? It's her house, too," Harry remarked. Was that why Sue had wanted a key to Harry's apartment? So she could drop by her own house unannounced, in the middle of the night, and still return to Harry's? Harry hadn't heard a thing — not that that made much difference. She had fallen into a deep sleep when she and Raven had finished making love, and it would have taken more than someone quietly coming and going past her bedroom to wake her up.

"Do you have any idea why Sue would sneak into your house?"

"No."

Manon's quiet response seized Harry's attention. What was Manon reluctant to tell her?

"Was anything missing?"

"Not that I could tell."

"Do you think she was looking for something and you interrupted her?"

Manon gave a slight shrug. "I haven't got a clue. If she wanted a change of clothes or some personal stuff but she didn't want to see me, she could have waited until I was at work. I have a fairly regular schedule. She didn't have to prowl around in her own house."

Harry nodded slowly. "But there's something you're not telling me, isn't there?"

Manon bit the corner of her lip and warily studied Harry. Then she reached into her purse, took out a folded sheet of paper and handed it to her. "I was worried that Sue had taken something from our office. We keep the originals of our deed, mortgage and other financial documents in one of the bottom desk drawers. I know they should be in a safety deposit box, but we've never got around to it. So after she rushed out, I went through the desk."

Harry unfolded the piece of paper. "Was anything missing?"

"No. But that letter was stuck between some other papers."

Harry glanced at the letter. Julie Beliveau's signature was scrawled across the bottom of the page. She quickly scanned the message. It was short, to the point and easily summarized: if Manon didn't leave Sue, Julie was going to tell her everything.

"Julie actually put her ultimatum in *writing?*"

"It looks like it. But I'm as surprised as you are. She never wrote me letters."

"And what about you? Did you send any to her?"

Manon made a face and then grimaced with pain. "Are you kidding? Francine would have noticed them in the mail. But I used to write sexy stuff and give it to her. She told me she destroyed it after she read it."

Harry raised her eyebrows. "And did she?"

"Do you think Julie would leave stuff like that lying around for Francine to find?"

Manon had a point.

"Listen, I swear to you that I never saw that letter from Julie before last night."

"So you think that Julie wrote it but never mailed it."

"Maybe," answered Manon.

"But how did Sue get her hands on it?"

Manon sighed. "Do you know what I really think? That Julie sent that letter to me but Sue intercepted it."

"Would Sue open an envelope addressed to you?"

"Maybe she did it by mistake," said Manon. "That happens, you know. I've done it myself. You get home from work, pick up the mail and automatically open everything without looking to see who it's addressed to."

Manon was right. Harry had done the same thing when she lived with Judy. What must Sue have thought when she read Julie's threat? And when had it been written? Harry looked at the letter, but it wasn't dated. She handed it to Manon, who refolded it and put it back in her purse.

"You know what Lieutenant-Detective Gagnon would do with that letter," Harry said.

Manon nodded. "Yes."

The question was, had Sue's intent been to plant the letter so that, when it was eventually found, Manon would skyrocket to the top of the list of suspects? But if she had wanted to retaliate against her unfaithful lover, why hadn't she simply given the letter to Gagnon? Perhaps Harry was reading it wrong. Maybe Sue had decided not to hand it over to the police and had returned it to the house instead. But why do that in the middle of the night? And why not put leave it in plain view on the kitchen counter or hall table?

"What are you going to do with the letter?" Harry asked.

"I should tear it up or flush it down the toilet. Or, better yet, burn it."

How could she countenance the destruction of that letter? It was evidence against both Manon and Sue. What if one of them had murdered Julie? "Why don't you give it to me for safekeeping?"

Manon gave a curt laugh. "You don't trust me, do you?" she said as she handed the letter to Harry, who tucked it in her purse.

"It's not that," Harry told her. "It would be wrong to destroy the letter, and you know it."

Manon reluctantly nodded. "You're right, of course. I feel like such a sucker, though. And Sue's going to feel bad when she sees my face."

If she sees her face, Harry thought. "Sue is staying with me now. She came by last night."

"I thought she was still at her sister's," Manon remarked. "Didn't you notice whether she went out during the night?"

"I was sleeping," Harry replied. She was somewhat confused about why Manon had showed up at her school in the middle of the day. At first she had naturally assumed that Manon had been beaten up and that she had no one else to turn to, but now it appeared that she had been hurt more or less accidentally, likely by Sue Phillips, and that she wasn't so much upset as annoyed about it. What did Manon want from her? "Why did you book off work to come see me?"

"I want you to arrange for me to talk to Sue," Manon replied.

"What makes you think I can do that?"

"She trusts you."

Harry finished her milkshake and put the glass down on the table. "Manon, do you think Sue murdered Julie?"

"Of course not!"

The look on Manon's face told Harry a different story. "She was angry enough to leave you, wasn't she? And to plant that letter on you."

"She's left me lots of times before. And how do you know she was intending to plant Julie's letter? Maybe she was giving it back."

Harry was beginning to get impatient with this now-you-see-me-now-you-don't routine. "Sue could have killed Julie, you know. She had a strong motive."

A stubborn look came over Manon's face, but that didn't stop Harry.

"Sue thought you had finally settled down. She was incensed when she found out that you and Julie were lovers. She lost respect for you because you were betraying both her and your sister," Harry said bluntly, undeterred when she saw the flash of anger on Manon's face. "What's the matter? Don't you like hearing the truth?"

"I thought you were my friend!"

"I am," Harry responded. "But you did a dumb thing, Manon, and now you're paying for it."

"Give me a break."

"Murderers don't give people breaks."

The waitress stopped at their booth. "Do you girls want anything else?"

"I'll have a coffee," Harry replied.

The waitress removed Harry's plate. "I'll bring the pot."

"Sue isn't the only person with a motive," Manon argued as soon as the waitress was out of earshot.

How well Harry knew that.

"As I told you before, I interrupted Sue and Julie out on the patio, and Sue went back inside the bar," Manon added. "Shortly after that, I went back into l'Entr'acte myself."

The waitress plunked a cup and saucer in front of Harry and filled the cup with coffee. Then she refilled Manon's cup and sat the nearly empty coffee pot on their table. She took her bill book from the pocket of her none-too-clean uniform, tore off the top bill and placed it beside the ketchup bottle. "Thanks, ladies."

"And you went to the front of the bar, didn't you? You wouldn't have noticed if Sue had gone out on the patio later to finish her argument with Julie. We both know that Julie would have got a great deal of satisfaction out of taunting Sue. You already told me that Sue was in a rage when you interrupted them. Don't you think that Sue could have become even angrier the more she thought about it, and returned to the patio to finish their argument? Sue could easily have lost control and killed her," Harry pointed out once the waitress had returned to the cash register.

"I can't believe you're talking to me like this about my lover," Manon said, shaking her head.

"And I think that there's still a lot you're not telling me."

"For instance?"

"You claimed that Sue didn't know about your relationship with Julie before you told her, when, in reality, you realized that she had somehow stumbled on the truth. That was why you 'confessed' when you did, isn't it? Sure, Julie gave you an ultimatum, but you could have put her off if you had really tried," Harry said.

"Is that the best you can do?"

"Why are you lying to me?"

Manon pulled a couple of dollars from her pocket and placed them on top of the bill. "That should cover my coffee. I thought you would be willing to help me, but it's clear that you've decided to take sides."

"I'm not taking anyone's side," Harry protested as Manon stood up, retrieved her coat and put it on.

"Oh yeah? Well, you could have fooled me," Manon said bitterly. "I'll see you around."

Harry watched her friend rush out of the café. The waitress glared at Harry as if Manon's black eye and the bruise on her cheek were Harry's fault.

The coffee in her cup was lukewarm, but she sipped it anyway. What was the matter with Manon? It wasn't like her to run away from her problems. Why was she so reluctant to tell the truth? And what made her think that Harry would have any success in convincing Sue to talk with her? Harry couldn't make rhyme or reason of her behaviour. Was Manon trying to protect someone — Sue, for instance — or had she murdered Julie herself? What did she really *know*?

And why had Sue gone home in the middle of the night? Had she planted Julie's letter or, as Manon claimed, returned it to its rightful owner? There was another possibility, of course. Manon could have been lying; the letter could have been in her desk drawer all along. Which didn't mean that Sue didn't know about it.

When she realized that she had come full circle, Harry finished her coffee and dropped some cash on the table. She ignored the look on the waitress's face and left the café.

The apartment was empty when Harry got home. She roamed through the rooms, feeling lonely. It was amazing how quickly she had grown used to Raven being there. Maybe what she felt was love. She wished she could decide. At any rate, she could easily imagine feeling a void in her life if Raven didn't come to Key West with her. Not that she had asked. Not yet, anyway.

Raven hadn't left a note, but Harry hadn't been due home for another two or three hours. Even so, she felt uneasy. She stopped herself from worrying; Raven was likely out shopping for dinner or exploring the neighbourhood. She put on a pot of decaffeinated coffee and checked the office; Sue's belongings were still there, her half-unpacked suitcase open on Harry's desk.

Harry dawdled in the kitchen until the coffee perked. She busied herself removing dishes from the drying rack and placing them in the cupboards and wiping the spots from the knives, forks and spoons before depositing them in the drawer. As soon as the pot stopped bubbling, she filled a mug, added milk and sugar, and carried it into the living room. She sat in the wing chair, put her mug on the table and stared out the window.

The house was chilly, especially in front of the bay window, which leaked cold air like a sieve. But Harry couldn't be bothered to rouse herself to turn up the heat. She was in a funk about Julie's murder. Everyone under the sun had a motive, some people more than one, and yet she couldn't make sense of it. The more she found out, the more confused she became. Too many people were telling partial truths, or worse, outright lies. How could she force the issue?

She was midway through her second cup of coffee when she heard the key turn in the lock. Sue Phillips walked in.

"You're home early," she said to Harry.

"So are you."

"I don't have a class last period on Tuesdays. I usually stay, but I wasn't in the mood today." Sue hung her coat in the closet and began walking toward the kitchen.

Harry got up, retrieved her mug and followed her. "There's a nearly full pot of coffee."

"I'd rather have a glass of water."

Harry refilled her mug one more time. "There's a jug of filtered water in the fridge."

Sue opened the fridge and removed the jug.

"Tell me, what were you and Julie talking about out on the patio the night she died?"

"I can't believe Manon blabbed!" Sue exclaimed.

Harry sat down at the table. "Would you like to talk to me about it?"

"Use your imagination, Harry. I told her off," Sue replied.

"Then what?"

"Manon interrupted me before I was finished. I was so angry that I went back inside the bar without saying anything else." Sue took a glass from the cupboard, filled it with water and sat down at the table.

"Why did you ask for a key to my apartment last night?" Harry asked.

"I don't like feeling that I can't leave."

"But it was after eleven."

"So?"

"Why did you go over to your house at three o'clock in the morning?"

Sue looked startled. "What are you talking about?"

"Manon told me she caught you sneaking around in the middle of the night."

"Manon's gone crazy then, because it sure as hell wasn't me."

"Well, somebody gave her a black eye and a huge bruise on her cheek."

"She got *beat up*?"

"Not exactly," Harry replied, explaining what had happened to Manon when she encountered the intruder.

"If that isn't the stupidest thing I've ever heard!"

"She could have been seriously hurt," Harry reminded her, an edge in her voice.

"You're right. But I assure you that it wasn't me," Sue said again. "I was right there in your office, stretched out on that incredibly uncomfortable trundle bed, trying to get a good night's sleep."

Harry didn't know whether to believe her or not.

"You've known me for years. Am I the type to skulk around my own house in the middle of the night?"

"Not really," Harry admitted. Although the person who had murdered Julie would likely resort to subterfuge to conceal his or her crime.

"Besides, if I had wanted to go home without seeing Manon, I would have gone during the day when she was at work," Sue asserted. "It's my house too, after all. I don't have any reason to sneak around."

"There wasn't anything you wanted to remove without Manon finding out that you had taken it?"

Sue looked at Harry as if she was crazy. "Like what? Manon is the one who keeps secrets, not me."

That was true. "And I suppose there wasn't anything you decided to leave there either?"

"What the hell are you talking about?" Sue said, losing her temper. "Do you always have to speak in riddles?"

The flush of anger on her face neatly matched the colour of her hair. For the first time, Harry could see the practicality of being a redhead.

"Well? Do you?"

Harry refused to be intimidated. "You didn't leave a letter in the desk?"

"What letter?"

Either Sue didn't know or she wasn't talking, so Harry changed topics. "How do you know so much about other people?"

Sue gave her a suspicious look. "Are you jerking me around? *What letter?*"

"Never mind about the letter. If you don't know, you don't know," Harry said. "But you seem to know a lot about what's going on. For example, you guessed about Manon and Julie before Manon told you."

"I've always been observant," Sue agreed. "Manon is the extrovert. She grabs everybody's attention and gets them going, while I sit back and watch. I find it amusing."

"So what else have you noticed?"

"About our friends, you mean? The people you suspect of having murdered Julie?"

Harry ignored Sue's irony and nodded.

"Marg Alexander was royally pissed off at Julie," Sue responded. "I don't know what the problem was. In fact, I hadn't realized until I saw them together this past weekend that they had stayed in touch with each other."

"Julie was after Marg's job in Toronto," said Harry. She didn't think it mattered if other people found out about it now that Julie was dead.

Sue looked shocked. "Talk about getting the lowdown on people."

"What else did you find out?" Harry asked, hoping Sue would decide to give her something in return for the information about Marg and Julie.

"Remember Saturday evening when I hinted to Francine that you and Julie were together?"

Harry nodded.

"Well, I realized then that she already knew about Manon and Julie."

"How did you figure that out?" Harry asked.

"Aren't you surprised?"

"No. Francine told me."

Sue looked annoyed. "I don't know why you're trying to pick my brain when you already know everything."

"How did you find out?"

"I thought Francine was jealous enough to believe anything about Julie. But when I first hinted around about you and Julie, Francine got this incredulous look on her face. I had only discovered Manon's betrayal the night before, so the shock of it was weighing on me. The pain was still close to the bone. But when Francine was reluctant to accept what I was insinuating, I began to wonder whether she was aware of Julie and Manon's affair."

"But in the end she did believe you, didn't she?"

"I thought so then, but now, I'm not really sure. I mean, if she knew about their relationship, she could have been playing along with me for the hell of it," Sue answered. "Perhaps she just wanted to put the fear of god in you. Or maybe she was bored and this was a welcome diversion. Francine can be a lot more devious than Manon, you know."

"I'll bet she can." Harry decided to return to the break-in. "About last night —"

Sue's temper flared again. "I told you, it wasn't me!"

"But Manon said she was certain it was you. She recognized the smell of your shampoo."

"Oh, come on. Am I the only person in the world who uses *Fleur d'esprit*? It's stocked in every pharmacy and half the grocery stores in the city. Tens of thousands of women buy it. And, as I told you, I was right here the whole damn night."

"I suppose you didn't break in here sometime Sunday, either," Harry remarked.

Sue blinked. "Was your house broken into?"

Harry heard the doorbell ring. In a way, she was relieved that this travesty of an interview was being interrupted, for it was evident that, if Sue knew anything, she wasn't going to tell. Harry got up and walked to the kitchen doorway, waving to Raven as she entered the apartment. She was laden with grocery bags. Marg Alexander followed her, lugging two large paper bags in her arms. Harry went to help them.

"You've been busy," she said to Raven once she had given her a kiss and relieved her of the bags.

"A family has to eat," Raven replied. "Phew! It's really cold out there." She shucked her winter coat, hung it in the closet and took the bags from Marg's arms so she could remove her jacket.

"Thanks for rescuing her," Harry said to Marg. She put Marg's jacket on a coat hanger and hung it beside Raven's.

"I was coming to see you anyway," Marg responded as Harry ushered them toward the kitchen. "I'm leaving tomorrow, so I thought I would say goodbye in person. I was supposed to get together with Sophie tonight, but it seems that there's something going on between her and Liz Martin."

"I was wondering about that," said Harry. "They dropped by last night on their way to dinner."

"It would be difficult to be in a relationship with someone in Quebec City," Marg commented. "Sophie is French, and she wouldn't want to move to Toronto. And I would never consider relocating to Quebec."

Sour grapes? Harry glanced at her, but Marg's face was expressionless.

"Well, I thought you looked good together," Harry said.

Marg gave an awkward laugh and fluffed her curly back hair with her hand. "So did I," she admitted. "But apparently Sophie wasn't ready to settle down. She told me that she's just coming off a relationship and that she needs time to get over it before she gets seriously involved with another woman. But we've all heard that before, haven't we?"

They assured Marg that indeed they had.

Sue stood up when the three of them entered the kitchen. "I think I'll rest for a little while."

Marg looked surprised to see her there. "You don't have to leave on my account."

Sue gave Marg an affectionate smile. "I'm not. I really am tired. You see, I didn't sleep well last night," she added, giving Harry an enigmatic look. "Call me before you leave, though."

"I will."

Sue disappeared around the corner and, seconds later, Harry heard the click of her office door closing. She put the bags down on the counter and said, "Have a seat. I'll make another pot of coffee."

Raven placed her grocery bags beside Harry's. "I'll be back in a minute. I've got a few things to rinse out in the bathroom sink."

Marg sat in the chair Sue had vacated. "She's certainly settled right in, hasn't she?"

"Yes." Harry took the can of decaffeinated coffee from the freezer and prepared a fresh pot of coffee. "I hope you don't mind if I unpack these grocery bags. I have no idea what she bought, and some things might need refrigerating."

"Go ahead," Marg answered. "I'd help if I didn't think I would be in the way."

"It will only take a minute." Harry began emptying the bags, placing everything on the counter. There was no meat, not that she had expected any. Raven was a vegetarian, and when they lived together in San Francisco, Harry had easily fallen into her lover's eating habits. There were bags of brown and red lentils, cans of chick peas and containers of various types of beans, which she placed in the cupboard; cartons of skim milk, tofu, yoghurt, sour cream and several small pieces of cheese, which she distributed on the shelves of the fridge; and bunches of fresh vegetables and bags of kiwi, oranges, grapefruit and peaches that she put in the vegetable crisper. She left the loaves of multigrain and fruit bread and whole-wheat rolls on the counter.

By the time she had folded the paper grocery bags and placed them in the recycling bin under the sink, the coffee had finished percolating. She filled a mug for Marg and put it on the table. Then she took an open carton of milk from the fridge. "Sorry I don't have any cream."

"I use milk anyway. But aren't you having any?"

"No," Harry answered as she sat down. "I've already had so many cups that I won't be able to sleep tonight as it is."

Marg added milk and sugar and stirred. "I wanted to stay for Julie's funeral, but Francine told me that she didn't know when it was going to be. The police haven't released the body yet, and they're apparently being rather coy about when they're going to."

"I suppose you have to get back to work."

"Yes. I've already used all my sick days, and I can't afford to lose pay, not when it looks as if I'll have to retire on a partial pension after this year. But most of all, I hate leaving before the killer is caught."

Harry could understand that. But didn't Marg realize that she was a suspect?

"Did you ever mention what you told me to Lieutenant-Detective Gagnon?" Harry asked.

"About Julie's attempt to usurp my job?"

"Yes."

"No. Why should I?"

"You know why."

Marg took a drink of coffee from her mug. "There's no law saying I have to turn myself into a suspect, especially when I didn't do it."

"You could have done it. You certainly had reason to, the way she double-crossed you. And you were at the bar that night, so you had the opportunity."

"Do you really think I would murder someone over a *job*?" Marg asked. "Someone else is going to take over when I leave, so Julie being dead doesn't change anything. Unemployed teachers are lined up behind those of us with positions; there's no lack of candidates to replace us the moment we're gone. What Julie did was underhanded, but even if she hadn't purposefully informed the head of the department that I was suffering from arthritis, he would have found out soon enough. Word gets around in a school environment, as you very well know. You can't keep a secret for long."

"But Julie plotted to get your job. People have killed for less," Harry pointed out.

Marg jumped up from the table, obviously angry. "I'm not some hypothetical 'person,' I'm someone you've known most of your adult life. And don't you forget it!"

"Marg —"

"I may have been angrier with Julie than I've ever been with anyone in my life, but *I didn't kill her*," Marg interrupted. "So from now on, I'll thank you to keep your nose out of my business."

Marg rushed from the kitchen. Harry started to follow her and then decided not to. When it came right down to it, she couldn't dismiss Marg Alexander as a suspect in Julie Beliveau's murder. Things didn't come easy to Marg. She was a plodder; intelligent, but a plodder nevertheless. Harry remembered their conversation in the woods during their Saturday afternoon excursion to the Laurentians, when Marg had bemoaned growing old alone, among other things. Harry had been frustrated by Marg's passivity, about her unwillingness to do something about her situation. Because she had to work so hard to get anywhere in life, Marg would resent anyone who ran interference. Marg would be capable of nursing a fierce hatred, and perhaps she would also be capable of acting violently on her feelings. Julie had taunted Marg, and she had been a constant provocation in her life. Julie wanted Marg's job, she had told Marg that she essentially had her job, but the union would protect Marg until arthritis made it impossible for her to continue working. In the end, it wouldn't be another teacher who would take away her job, it would be her physical disability. Intellectually, Marg knew that; the question was, did she accept it emotionally?

The front door slammed. Harry belatedly remembered that Sue had wanted to see Marg before she left. Well, it was too late now. Sue would have to call her.

As for Harry, she decided that it would be better to wait until Marg was home in Toronto and had the opportunity to calm down before attempting to speak to her again. They had been friends for years, and Harry hoped that eventually they would be again.

anon arrived just after Raven had served the rice and lentil stew she had prepared the day before. Harry had pulled the table away from the wall to make space for herself, Raven and Sue, and Sue was trapped behind it when Manon stormed into the kitchen. She stopped in front of the table and placed her hands on her skinny hips.

"I want to talk to you," she said to Sue.

"Your face!" exclaimed Sue.

"Never mind about my face," Manon said curtly. "I want to talk to you."

Raven put down the knife she had been using to carve thick slices of multigrain bread. "Perhaps we should leave them alone," she said to Harry.

But Harry wanted to hear what Manon had to say to her girlfriend.

"Why don't you join us for dinner?" Harry asked Manon. "Otherwise everything will get cold."

"You can talk after dinner," added Raven.

"*Bon*," Manon said once she realized that this would further aggravate Sue. "Fine."

Harry retrieved a fourth chair from the office, removing a pair of Sue's jeans and a ragged nightgown from it before lugging it into the kitchen.

"Haven't you got any wine?" Manon asked once she was settled at the table.

"There's apple cider," answered Raven.

"*Bon*."

"But it's non-alcoholic," Raven added.

"Forget it, then. I'll just have coffee."

Harry handed her the pot.

"I suppose it's decaffeinated, too."

"That's right," replied Harry.

Raven's rice and lentil stew was spicy, the bread fresh, the salad covered with a tangy dressing, but the level of tension at the table was so high that it was difficult to enjoy dinner. Sue was the first to surrender, perhaps because Manon was seated across from her, an unrelenting scowl on her face.

Sue dropped her spoon in her stew and leaned back. "What do you want?"

Go on, say it, Harry mentally urged Manon. Say what you mean and get this over with. Say "you." Say I want *you*.

Manon took her time. She licked her spoon clean and put it down beside her plate. She reached to the counter to retrieve the coffee pot and emptied the dregs into her cup. Harry was ready to crawl under the table and bite her ankle by the time Manon spoke.

"Did you kill her?"

Sue threw a piece of bread at her lover. Since she had been the ace pitcher of the university's softball team and since she had gone on to star in every dyke league in which she had pitched, the bread hit Manon squarely on the forehead. Sue had already buttered it, so it stuck.

Raven burst out laughing, which set Harry off.

Manon reached up, removed the bread from her forehead and then wiped away the butter with a napkin. "Was that a yes or a no?"

Sue started to laugh and then thought the better of it. "Did *you* kill her?" she asked suddenly.

"Get serious," Raven muttered. She helped herself to more rice and lentil stew and passed the serving bowl to Sue, who handed it to Harry.

"Who do you think killed her?" Manon asked Raven.

"I have my ideas," Raven said. "And so do the two of you, apparently. It must be hard to suspect your lover. Very painful, I would imagine."

Harry had to hand it to Raven; the pervasive sense of hilarity was gone in an instant.

Manon's head dipped, as if she was ashamed of herself. "I don't really think that Sue killed Julie."

"I don't believe that you did either," Sue murmured. "And I'm sorry I threw bread at you."

"Better bread than stew," Manon said, a hint of a smile crossing her thin lips. "I don't understand why you broke into the house just to leave me that letter, though. You could have come by while I was at work and I never would have known."

"As I keep telling everyone, I *didn't break into our house!*" Sue balled her paper napkin and tossed it on the table. "I've still got a key, and I have more pride than to sneak around in the middle of the night. I can't say that I had a good sleep, but I didn't leave this apartment that night. And what letter are you talking about?"

"But your shampoo —"

"My shampoo be damned," Sue interrupted. "*Fleur d'esprit* is one of the most common shampoos around. Francine said —"

The phone rang. Harry pushed back her chair and answered it.

"Harry, it's Judy. Did you tell that damn cop that I had an affair with Julie?"

Harry opened her mouth to reply and then realized that she didn't want to talk to Judy with an audience of three paying close attention. "Hold on — let me take this in my office."

She mouthed the word "Judy" as she handed the receiver to Raven, who made a face. Harry gave her a silent kiss on the forehead and went into the office. She eventually found her telephone buried under a pile of clothes. She picked it up and said, "It's okay, Raven. You can hang up now."

"Don't be long, darling," Raven whispered, her voice sultry.

There was a quiet click.

That little devil. Harry could sense Judy's blood pressure rising. "Now, what were you saying?"

"Christ! I can't believe you've shacked up with that woman!"

"That's none of your business, and if you want me to stay on the line you had better get off that topic altogether," Harry warned her.

There was a momentary silence, and then Judy began speaking again, her tone chilly. "What precisely did you tell that detective about me?"

"Lieutenant-Detective Gagnon?"

"Himself."

At least she could answer truthfully, Harry thought. "I didn't say anything about you."

"Then how did he know about my relationship with Julie?"

"I would imagine that he has his own ways of finding things out," Harry responded, her interest piqued by the detective's discovery. She was impressed. He must have really been digging. She wondered what else he had managed to find out. "Has he been accusing you of committing murder?"

"Of course not!"

"Well, don't be surprised if he does. It's his job to suspect everyone involved in the case, after all."

"I'm not *involved*."

"You could have fooled me," Harry remarked. "You certainly had a motive, and you were at the bar the night she died."

"You know, Harry, you're a first-class bitch," Judy remarked, her tone bitter. "Not only that, you're disloyal to your friends."

Not all that long ago, Harry would have been hurt by what Judy said. She would have felt guilty and blamed herself. But not anymore. Those days were over. "You're not my friend."

There was a shocked silence.

"See, friends don't betray each other, and that's what you did to me," Harry added. "Now, if you're finished, I've got company." She hung up without waiting for Judy to reply and then threw herself on the unmade trundle bed. It threatened to collapse, but didn't. Harry turned on her back and stared at the ceiling, which was covered with hairline cracks and needed a coat of paint. It gave her a certain sense of satisfaction to realize that it would be up to the next tenant to harass the landlord to plaster and paint and maintain the flat in good repair.

Where had all that anger come from? She had certainly kept it under wraps for a long time, so long that she hadn't realized it was there. She should have controlled her temper; Judy was a suspect, and Harry had just blown any possibility of questioning her. She should have played it cool and sympathized with her ex-lover's tribulations. Lieutenant-Detective Gagnon could be quite a pain in the ass, after all.

Harry closed her eyes. The problem was that she didn't really believe that Judy had killed Julie. During the last two years of their relationship, she had discovered that Judy was ethically spineless. She had taken liberties with Harry's trust. She had tried to make Harry accept non-monogamy. But that didn't mean she had murdered someone.

That left Manon, Sue, Isabelle, Marg, Albert and Francine on Harry's list of suspects. Two of them were sitting at her kitchen table right now, but fat lot of good it was doing her. Why was she having so much trouble getting people to tell the truth?

She had to stop doubting herself. If she didn't follow her instincts, she was never going to solve this crime. She opened her eyes and sat up. Of the six remaining suspects, Isabelle Lachance and Albert Dack were the least likely to have murdered Julie Beliveau. If she could disarm Isabelle and Albert, maybe they would stop being so defensive. Yeah, and if cows could fly, Harry mused. Albert Dack was one of the most prickly people Harry had ever had the misfortune to meet. And his wife wasn't much better.

She got up and searched through the top drawer of her desk until she came across her address book. She found Isabelle and Albert's phone number and dialled it. Their answering machine came on after four rings. Harry didn't bother to leave a message; she was certain they wouldn't return her call.

What next? Francine? But she had already questioned the dead woman's lover on several occasions, and each time Francine had managed to slip through her fingers. Still, it was worth a try. She located Francine's number and dialled.

Isabelle Lachance answered the telephone.

"Oh, hi, Isabelle," Harry said. "Is Francine around?"

"She's taking a nap," Isabelle responded, her tone guarded. "Why?"

"I just thought I would see how she was," Harry fibbed. She had no intention of giving either of the Lachance sisters an attempt to elude her.

"She's about as well as can be expected," Isabelle replied.

What the hell did that mean? And what was Harry supposed to say? "That's good. Listen, don't disturb her on my account," Harry said even though she knew Isabelle had no such intention. "Just tell her I called and that I'll speak to her tomorrow."

"Fine."

The line went dead. So much for loosening Isabelle up.

Harry put her address book back in the desk drawer. It was way past time to rescue Raven from Manon and Sue. Harry just hoped the two lovebirds weren't at each other's throats again.

She left the office and went back into the kitchen, but it was empty. She could hear voices coming from the hall, so she walked toward them.

Sue was putting on her jacket. "So you've finally resurfaced. I was beginning to think that you had settled in for the night."

"That was an awfully long call," remarked Manon. She was already wearing her coat and scarf.

There was no point in telling Manon and Sue about Judy's affair with Julie. Despite Judy's miserable attitude, that would remain her and Harry's sordid little secret now that Julie was dead. "Judy told me off."

"She's got some nerve," Raven blurted.

Harry put her arm around Raven's waist and hugged her. "Never mind. Are you leaving already?" she asked Manon.

"As soon as Sue collects her stuff."

Manon and Sue went to the office, leaving Harry and Raven standing just inside the front door. Harry looked out the bay window and saw that it was snowing again.

"So they made up."

"I wouldn't exactly say that, but Sue did agree to return home," Raven replied. "She claims that your trundle bed is barely a step up from sleeping on nails."

"Oh, come on — it's not that bad."

"I'm sure not, but it does give her a way to save face."

"You mean they're not really talking."

"I'm not certain they'll be able to, at least not for a while," Raven said. "I think everything will blow up in their faces if they tackle things too soon. Both of them feel too hurt to face the truth. Especially Sue."

Harry was about to reply when Sue and Manon returned from the office. Manon was carrying one suitcase and Sue the other, but she didn't look excited about going home. There was no glimmer of hope in Manon's eyes, either. Raven was right; they were both in pain. Harry feared for their relationship.

"We're off, then," Sue said, giving Harry a hug.

Harry hugged her back. "If you need me —"

Sue's hands squeezed her shoulders. "I know where you are."

"You, too," Harry added as Manon kissed both of her cheeks.

"*Bien sûr*. Sure," Manon said. "*Bonsoir*, Raven."

"Goodnight."

"I wouldn't want to be in their shoes," Raven remarked once the door closed behind them. "They've got a hell of a lot of stuff to work through, haven't they? And one of them might have murdered Julie."

"And as long as they suspect each other, they aren't going to be able to concentrate on solving the problems they're having in their relationship."

"It's all Manon's fault," Raven said as she wrapped her arms around Harry.

"Most of it," Harry agreed, distracted when Raven ran her hands up and down her back. Her fingers cupped Harry's behind and pulled her close.

"*Most* of it? Harry, your pal Manon has been cheating on her girlfriend since the word go," Raven pointed out. "If I were Sue, I would have broken up with her long ago."

"So you believe in monogamy, do you?"

Raven tucked her face in Harry's neck and gently bit her. "What do you think?"

The fact that Harry didn't know was more than a little disquieting, especially since her longest relationship had so recently ended because of a dispute over that very matter.

"Actually, I'm not sure."

"Let me give you a hint: Every bone in my body is jealous," Raven whispered in her ear. "And that's quite a few bones." She began to lick Harry's earlobe.

Harry was beginning to get the message. Both messages, in fact. Her body grew warm with desire, but she didn't succumb. She still had two more suspects to question, and both of them were at Francine Lachance's flat. She gave Raven a fierce hug.

"That doesn't feel very horny to me," Raven remarked, tilting her head and studying Harry.

"You know how much you turn me on," Harry reassured her. "But I want to drop by Francine's before it gets late. I won't be long, though."

"I'll be here."

Harry kissed her. Some time later, when Raven could have no doubt about how strongly she was attracted to her, Harry reluctantly broke away, put her coat and boots on and went out. One of these days she was going to have to make up her mind just what her intentions were about Raven. But this damn murder investigation was always getting in the way.

sabelle opened the door. "*Toi!* You!"

Harry frowned. "Were you expecting someone else?"

"Albert," Isabelle answered. "He's supposed to pick me up, and he's late."

"It's snowing again, so perhaps the traffic is bad. Can I come in?"

"What do you want?"

"To talk to you," Harry responded. "And to Francine."

Isabelle was obviously reluctant to let her in, but she stood aside to let Harry pass. "Thanks."

"I'm warning you, I haven't got anything to say."

Harry went into the living room, dropped her coat on the arm of one of the leather sofas and sat down.

"I wonder about that," she mused. "You've known Manon and Francine longer than anyone else. You lived in the same house with them, you played with them, grew up with them. You've always been a close family."

"That's true," Isabelle agreed.

Harry wondered just how intimate the three sisters had been as adults. Had the twins known about Isabelle's short affair with a female classmate? "Did you tell Manon or Francine about your relationship with a woman when you were in university?"

Isabelle sat down on the other leather sofa. "*Merde!* Of course I didn't! Listen, it wasn't all that important, so why would I have mentioned it to my sisters? You're making a mountain out of a molehill. My what you call a 'relationship' lasted only a couple of months from start to finish."

"I take it you didn't want to be gay."

Isabelle pursed her lips while she studied Harry. "Manon and Francine were very influential when I was younger. They were my only siblings, and essentially they raised me. Our mother didn't mind. She was relieved when they were old enough to babysit, to take me to and from school, to help me with my homework, to amuse me on weekends. When she realized they were capable of looking after me, she went out and got a job. My parents needed the money. It made a difference: It meant having fresh food on the table and some new clothes once in a while. I can't think when I first figured out that the twins were gay; when I look back, it seems that I always knew, although that's probably impossible. In any case, their lesbianism was a given, not something out of the ordinary."

"So it was only natural for you to experiment with it yourself."

Isabelle nodded. "*C'est vrai.* I can see that now, although when it happened, I was shocked. I dated boys in high school, although I didn't have much sexual experience when I started university. My mother put the fear of God in me about getting pregnant and ruining my life, not to mention hers, so I was deathly afraid of letting boys touch me. I was quite inexperienced sexually when my classmate began flirting with me. I didn't even know what was going on until, one night, she started making love to me."

Harry didn't think anyone could be *that* innocent, but she wasn't going to contradict whatever rationalizations Isabelle had constructed to separate that part of her life from the rest. "So you couldn't deal with it, despite the fact that you grew up with two sisters who were gay."

"It didn't feel right," Isabelle professed. "Not the way it did for Manon and Francine. I was different, I guess. I didn't want to live that kind of life."

"And Albert never found out," Harry said, letting her scepticism show.

"I told you before and I'll tell you again, the only thing he knows is that she had a crush on me," Isabelle insisted.

"And you've never felt guilty about this deception?"

"Why should I? I didn't tell him about what I did with the boys I dated in high school, so why should I have said anything about her? Albert was the first person I had sexual relations with, and that certainly overshadowed everything else," replied Isabelle.

Harry didn't agree, but she wasn't about to argue, although it was clear that, despite the accommodations Isabelle had made to keep her past at bay, it had caught up with her anyway. "You didn't answer my first question: Did your sisters know?"

"No. I was very careful. I didn't want them to be disappointed or to feel that I was prejudiced when I turned my back on their lifestyle."

"Then how did Julie find out?"

"I don't know," Isabelle maintained. She was beginning to sound agitated.

"It's okay," Harry said in a soothing voice. "But was Julie trying to blackmail you or not?"

"No. But Julie didn't like me. And she didn't like Albert. She didn't want us around, partly because we weren't gay, partly because she hated it when anyone was closer to Francine than she was."

Harry could see the truth in that. Julie had played hard to get until she became involved with Francine. Then she became possessive in the extreme, despite her flirtatious posturing toward other women. Inconsistent, perhaps, but not when seen in a certain light. "Go on."

"She acted as if Alfred was a piece of dirt under her foot, but he tolerated it for my sake," Isabelle said.

Julie had not been a nice person. And Albert wasn't exactly the most sociable — or likable — person. "So nothing was ever said about your relationship with a woman."

"Or about a lot of other things, either," Isabelle said succinctly. "Anyway, I certainly didn't kill Julie, and neither did Albert. Sure, we were at a nearby café the night she was killed, but we didn't realize that Julie was at the bar. And if we had known, we wouldn't have cared. If you want to know the truth, I never really thought that Julie would go so far as to tell Albert or my vice-principal about what happened."

"But what if she did?"

"I would have simply denied it," Isabelle contended. "I've been married to Albert for twenty years. Whom would he believe, me or Julie?"

It would make for good gossip, but she was undoubtedly right: In the end, people would conclude that Isabelle was straight and that Julie was telling malicious lies, for whatever the reason. Albert might have his doubts, but he was unlikely to dissolve a twenty-year relationship over such old news.

Another thought occurred to Harry. "How long ago did Julie tell you that she knew?"

"Let me see," Isabelle mused. "She started dropping hints last winter, and then one evening at a party at Manon's this past spring, I confronted her about it."

Even more reason to believe that Isabelle was innocent. If she had been terrified that Julie was going to inform on her, she would have killed her then, not six or seven months later. And Harry's notion that Albert was the guilty party was even more implausible. It would indicate that he knew about his wife's affair with a woman and had killed Julie to protect Isabelle's reputation. Of course, Julie could have told him, but Harry didn't think so. Julie was devious enough to want to have something to hold over Isabelle, and telling Albert would take away from that.

There were footsteps on the interior stairs, and seconds later Albert walked into the living room. He had removed his boots, but he was still wearing his long, grey coat. Snow was melting on his shoulders.

"*Bonsoir*, Harriet."

"*Bonsoir*," Harry replied.

Isabelle shot her a warning glance. "I suppose we should be going."

"*Oui*," Albert answered. "I want to get home before it starts snowing any harder."

"Is Francine sleeping?" Harry asked as Isabelle rose from the sofa.

"She was when I left her," Isabelle said. "Are you planning to stick around?"

"For a while."

"I won't disturb her, then. When she wakes up, tell her I'll be over tomorrow after school."

"I will."

Harry made desultory conversation with the two of them while Isabelle donned her winter clothes. She closed the door behind them, secured the lock and went back into the living room. Her search was narrowing; Isabelle and Albert were nearly out of the running as suspects. She had to question Francine before she could go further.

She walked through the dining room toward the bedroom to see if Francine was awake. As she passed the bathroom, she saw that the light was on, so she detoured, intending to turn it off. The bathroom had benefited greatly from Julie's renovation. She had knocked out the wall and extended the room so that a jacuzzi bathtub could be installed. The primitive sink and toilet had been replaced, floor-to-ceiling tile had been laid, and plush-looking but industrial-strength carpet covered the floor.

Harry was about to switch off the light when a plastic bottle standing on the edge of the tub caught her eye. She padded silently across the carpet and picked up the half-empty plastic bottle, her mind racing. It was *Fleur d'esprit* shampoo.

"Planning to take a shower?" Francine asked.

Harry dropped the bottle and wheeled around. Francine was leaning against the doorjamb, her arms crossed. She was dressed in jeans, a black turtleneck and a navy suede jacket.

Harry laughed, her voice cracking. She made an effort to overcome the fear that suddenly rushed through her, and bent and retrieved the bottle of *Fleur d'esprit* from where it had fallen on the carpet.

"Not until I get home," she answered. "I just came in here to turn out the light, and then I noticed this," she said, holding up the bottle. "The other day, at school, someone mentioned that it was a great shampoo, and cheap too. I was just going to smell it to see if I liked it."

"Go ahead, then."

"What?"

"Smell it," Francine said.

Harry opened the bottle, put it lip to her nose and sniffed. "Very subtle."

"Isn't it, though."

"You must be wondering how I got in," Harry said, stalling for time. She screwed the cap back on the bottle of *Fleur d'esprit*. Francine used the same shampoo as Sue Phillips. Manon had smelled *Fleur d'esprit* on the person who broke into her house. Was it just a coincidence, or had Francine been the intruder? And if so, what did that mean? Why had she been sneaking around Manon and Sue's house in the middle of the night? Had Julie written a letter of ultimatum to Manon and then never mailed it, a letter that Francine discovered and then hid in the drawer of Manon's desk? Harry put the bottle of shampoo on the edge of the tub.

"Isabelle let me in after you fell asleep. Albert picked her up a couple minutes ago."

"I wasn't asleep, but it doesn't matter. Listen, I was just about to have a beer. Care to join me?"

Harry's good sense told her to leave now, but she couldn't bear to go. She was like a dog worrying a bone. "Sure."

"Come on, then."

Harry followed her to the kitchen, telling herself that everything was all right. She was just going to have a beer with Francine and ask her a few questions.

"Isabelle said she would drop by after school tomorrow," Harry said once they were seated at the kitchen table. It was covered with a tablecloth which looked new but cheap. Harry looked around while Francine opened the refrigerator and removed two bottles of beer. There were other changes, too: Several magnets adhered to the fridge door; an ashtray containing several cigarette butts rested on the far edge of the table; and the stale smell of cigarette smoke polluted the air. A lighter and a pack of Gitanes sat beside the ashtray.

Francine twisted off the cap and put a bottle in front of Harry. "Did you chase her away with all your questions?"

"Isabelle is not easily deterred," Harry replied.

Francine snorted. She removed the cap from the bottle in her hand and sat down. "Neither are you, it would seem."

Their eyes met. Francine's were cold enough to make Harry shiver. It was then that the pieces began to fall into place. It had been Francine who had broken into her house, not to steal anything, but to write "Stop asking questions!" on her bathroom mirror. Perhaps she was protecting someone else, Harry thought. Then she realized that she was grasping at straws. There was no one to protect. There was only one reason why Francine would leave her that message, and that was because she had murdered her lover.

"Why?"

The only sign of acknowledgement Francine gave was the slight elevation of one eyebrow. She lifted her bottle to her mouth and took a long drink of beer without breaking eye contact with Harry.

"Why? Were you jealous about her relationship with Manon?"

"You've got an overactive imagination," Francine said with a grin meant to be disarming.

But Harry wasn't having any. "Or was it because you wanted this building? It's worth a lot of money, after all. You could sell it, buy a condo and stop working at l'Entr'acte if you managed your finances carefully."

The grin was replaced by a look of unrepentant hostility. "Back off, Hubbley."

She was getting closer. "You lived with Julie for five years, and she changed her will shortly after you moved in. Then she and Manon started having an affair a couple of years ago. So why now and not then?"

"I said back off!" Francine was angry. She finished her beer, slammed the empty bottle on the table and lit a cigarette. Acrid smoke swirled around her head.

"You found out that Julie wanted to move to Toronto, didn't you? And that she was going to leave you behind. I imagine she was in love with you in the beginning. You likely fascinated her because the two of you were so different. But she soon grew tired of your jealousy, and you couldn't — or wouldn't — change. She enjoyed teasing you and making you lose your temper. I could see that last Friday evening when she came on to me. That was for your benefit, not mine. She wanted to get a rise out of you, and you performed up to her expectations. But essentially she was bored with the scenes you created."

"Go to hell!"

"How did you find out? Did you eavesdrop when she was on the phone with Marg Alexander? I bet that's what happened. Once you realized that Julie was going to move to Toronto, you knew it was only a matter of time before she wrote you out of her will. Because as soon as everything was in place, she was going to leave you, wasn't she? Otherwise, she would have told you about her plans. She would have included you in them and asked you to relocate with her. But she didn't. She wasn't sure she wanted Manon to go to Toronto with her either, even though she tried to get her to leave Sue."

Francine didn't have anything to say this time.

"If I can figure it out, so can Lieutenant-Detective Gagnon," Harry said softly.

Francine blew smoke at her. "*C'est vrai*. It's true. He's not as stupid as I first thought he was, and neither are you. You know, I never really liked you, Hubbley. When I first met you, I found you tiresome. You always depended on my sister to make your life exciting, and you haven't changed much over the years. Whenever you get too close to the edge, you run away. You want to be safe."

Well, she wasn't running now, was she? Although it might have been prudent to get out rather than sit there exchanging insults with a murderer. "We're not talking about me, Francine. We're talking about you and the fact that you killed Julie. Why don't you tell me about it?"

Francine got up and opened the fridge door again. She took out another bottle of beer, closed the door and leaned against it. "It's pretty much as you said," she replied with a resigned shrug. She uncapped the bottle and drank. "I tried to tell myself that I didn't care about her affair with Manon, but it wasn't true. It was eating me up inside. But I didn't know what to do about it, partly because they didn't realize that I knew. Perhaps if I could have confronted them — but for once in my life, I couldn't. My sister, my own twin sister, double-crossing me with my own lover! I couldn't believe it."

"I can understand that," Harry said. As soon as the words were out of her mouth, she realized she had made a mistake. Francine didn't need any encouragement, she was already angry.

One corner of Francine's mouth turned up in a humourless smile. She finished her second beer and placed the empty bottle on the table. "She was always taunting me, always," Francine hissed. "I knew it didn't mean a damn thing, but everyone could see how she treated me. I felt humiliated."

Harry felt queasy. Her mouth was dry, but she didn't touch her beer. "So once you killed Julie, you decided to frame Manon for her murder. You went to Manon's last night to plant the letter in her office, didn't you? You wanted Lieutenant-Detective Gagnon to find out about Julie and Manon's affair. You might have even been planning to help him reach that conclusion by dropping a few hints."

Francine laughed. "I had more than hints to offer him. It seems that Manon writes pretty good love letters, sex and all."

Julie had not been as careful as Manon thought she was, Harry reflected. Otherwise, she would have destroyed Manon's missives. "Manon thought you were Sue because you both use the same shampoo. Manon gave it to you for Christmas last year, didn't she?"

Francine took another beer from the fridge.

"You weren't planning to kill Manon, were you?"

"No, dammit!" Francine shouted. She spun about and threw the bottle at Harry.

"Shit!" Harry recoiled backwards. The bottle slammed into the wall. It smashed, spattering her with beer and shards of glass. The pungent smell of beer saturated the air. Her chair teetered on its back legs and then went over. Harry ignored the sharp pain that blossomed in her right shoulder and hip and scrabbled to her knees.

"I wanted to kill them both! Those bitches deserved it! But I wouldn't kill Manon no matter what she did. She's my *sister*. Don't you understand?" Francine yelled. She moved closer and kicked Harry's overturned chair.

Harry scrambled out of the way. She was pressed against the back door. She planted her feet on the glass-strewn floor and slowly pushed herself into an upright position. The room reeked of beer and cigarette smoke and extreme danger.

"Calm down, Francine," she said, trying to sound composed. "It's over. It's all *over*."

Francine was breathing heavily. "I loved Julie, but it was never enough. I was going insane with jealousy. That night at the bar, Sue said Julie was with you, and that set me off. I didn't really believe it, I was positive she was with Manon, but I wasn't sure about anything to do with Julie anymore. Manon and Julie arrived at the bar separately, but I knew they had been together, that they had been making love in the back seat of a car or in some grimy motel room. I could always see it in Julie's face or smell it on her skin. The way she looked at Manon disgusted me. I was so mad I didn't know what to do with myself."

If Francine would just keep talking, Harry was sure she could find a way to escape. "Then Julie went out on the patio, and you waited until Sue and then Manon came back inside," she surmised.

"Yes. I had made up my mind to confront her, to tell her that I had found out about everything, that I knew all about her affair with Manon and her plans to leave me and move to Toronto," Francine replied.

"And did you?"

Francine nodded. "I begged her to stay, but she laughed at me."

"So you picked up the brick and hit her with it."

"I *loved* her," Francine whispered. "I didn't mean to kill her, but I'd been so angry for so long. And I couldn't let her leave me."

Harry exhaled slowly. "Then you decided to frame Manon."

Francine's face hardened. "I couldn't kill her. I wanted to, but I couldn't. We were like two peas in a pod when we were kids. We could nearly read each other's minds. I would start a sentence and she would finish it. Our mother dressed us alike. That was how things were done in those days. The teachers sat us together all through elementary school. When I was little, I thought everybody had a twin, somebody who was just like them. I never thought she would betray me. I went to her house last night, but I didn't break in. I had a key, you see. She gave me one shortly after she and Sue bought the place, but that was so long ago that I'm sure she forgot about it. I put Julie's letter in Manon's desk, under a bunch of papers. I was going to 'find' Manon's letters to Julie and give them to the police. When they realized that Manon and Julie were lovers, they would have gone after Manon, searched her house, found Julie's letter and arrested her."

"But Manon heard you and came downstairs. What happened then?" Harry asked. She eased closer to the edge of the door, casually placing one hand behind her. It grazed and then settled on the doorknob. Harry had no way of knowing whether the door was locked, but being close to an escape route made her feel less panicky.

"I put my head down and ran like hell," Francine said. "I didn't stop when I ran into her. Even though she went down, I knew she wasn't hurt badly."

"I didn't think you were capable of killing your sister," commented Harry.

"C'est vrai," Francine agreed, suddenly amiable. "You're right. But I'm sure ready to kill you."

Harry closed her hand around the doorknob. The inside door opened easily. She fumbled with the latch of the aluminum storm door and got it open. Francine began to laugh as Harry stepped through the doorway onto the snow-covered balcony.

"Where do you think you're going? This is the third floor." Francine sounded genuinely amused.

Harry slammed the storm door, but there was no way to lock it from the outside. She braced her stockinged feet against the snow-covered deck and leaned against the door.

"Have it your way," Francine said with a laugh. "See if I care if you freeze to death."

Harry heard the metallic clang of the bolt shooting home and then Francine closed the inner door. Harry had a few moments' respite, but she knew that Francine wouldn't leave her alone for long. She wasn't the type to leave things to chance. She would likely wait until Harry was weak from the cold so she could easily finish her off.

Harry looked over the railing. She was on the third floor, and it was a hell of a long way down to the freshly plowed courtyard below. She wrapped her arms around her body and shivered in the frosty air. The wind had picked up and snow was falling. Her feet were already aching from the cold. It was either escape or die. Under the circumstances, the thought that Francine would never get away with it was little consolation.

"HELP!" she screamed several times, but it seemed pointless. None of the windows in the courtyard was lit and it was unlikely anyone on boulevard St-Joseph would hear her. And if she made too much noise, Francine would return sooner rather than later. She looked down again, squinting in the dark at the two-by-fours that supported the balcony. Could she?

Harry's toes were numb and her bare hands were stiffening. If she didn't attempt to escape now, her body would shortly be too sluggish from the cold to try. She eased one leg and then the other over the railing, her toes fighting for purchase on the slippery edge of the balcony as she lowered her hands one at a time. Once she had wrapped herself around the two-by-four, the rest was relatively easy. The hardest part was controlling the speed of her descent on the slick wood. She reached the second balcony and repeated her movements and, before long, she was on the ground.

She ran stiffly from the empty courtyard and followed the lane to boulevard St-Joseph, making straight for the telephone booth on the corner.

Harry sorted through another stack of books and put most of them in the pile to be shipped to Key West.

Raven paused in packing books into a cardboard carton. "You're hardly giving any away."

"But they're my *books*," Harry protested.

"They're also very heavy," Raven pointed out. "Stop being so stubborn. You can buy whatever books you want once you get settled in Key West."

Harry knew that was true, but she was reluctant to leave her books behind. Sometimes she thought that the more she took, the less likely she would be to get homesick and the longer she would stay in Key West. Besides, she had the money to move everything she wanted to. She was simply using this opportunity to cull her possessions.

"All this work is making me thirsty," Raven announced, running her hand over the hair on top of her head. "Do you want something to drink?"

"Just water," Harry replied. She watched Raven pad from the room. She was wearing her ubiquitous black tights topped with a heavy green sweater of Harry's which reached halfway down her thighs. She had a thick pair of woollen socks on her feet and a colourful scarf wrapped around her neck, and she looked so cute that Harry wanted to hold her and never let go. Instead, she sat back, leaned against a pillar of packed boxes and closed her eyes.

She was exhausted. She hadn't said anything to Raven, but she hadn't been able to sleep for the better part of a week now, not since last

Tuesday evening. Shortly after she had made her phone call, a police car had pulled up to the curb, its siren blaring. One of the patrolmen rushed to the telephone booth and whisked her into the relative warmth of the car. She insisted on accompanying them to Francine Lachance's third-floor apartment, even though the police didn't want her to. Perhaps Francine would surrender peacefully, she told them, and the two young constables conceded her point. They called for back-up, and a second patrol car arrived just as Harry and the two uniformed policemen entered the building. She was wrapped in one of the constable's jackets, a pair of large rubber boots on her feet.

"Here's your water," Raven said.

Harry started.

Raven managed to hold onto the glass, but some of the water spilled on the floor.

"It's all right," Harry whispered.

"No, it's not," Raven replied. She sat down beside Harry and took her in her arms. "You're trembling. Have you been taking those sleeping pills your doctor prescribed?"

"I don't need them."

"Yes, you do." Raven kissed her forehead and began rocking her. "I wish you would tell me about it."

"There's not much to tell," Harry sniffed. "She was dead when we got there. I like to think that she was trying to escape, but, in my heart, I know it's not true. When she realized I was gone, she threw herself off the balcony. Poor Francine. She wanted to die. It was too much for her."

"How can you feel sympathy for her? She was going to kill you," Raven said.

"Maybe, maybe not," Harry prevaricated. But she knew what Raven said was true. Francine was going to murder her as thoughtlessly as she would have swatted a fly.

Raven was silent for a while. "What's going to happen to the rest of them?"

"I spoke to Manon for a minute after the funeral yesterday when you went to the parking lot to get the car," Harry replied. "She's put in for a leave of absence until after the holidays."

"She must be pretty miserable."

"She's taking it very hard. Despite everything, she and Francine were close. But more than anything else, I think she feels guilty."

"I hope so. It was her fault that Francine murdered Julie."

Harry was surprised at the vehemence in Raven's voice. "Manon didn't make Francine kill Julie," she gently pointed out. "Violence never solves problems people have in their relationships."

"I know," conceded Raven. "But what Manon did was so wrong."

"I think she knows that now. And Sue left her again," Harry said. "She called me at work yesterday and said she wasn't going to attend the funeral because she didn't want to see Manon. She resigned from her job with two weeks' notice, and apparently she's moving to Toronto in the new year. She's been in touch with Marg Alexander, who invited her to stay with her until she gets settled."

"I'm not surprised that she doesn't want to live with Manon," Raven said. "I couldn't live with someone so immoral either."

"Sue told me that she wants to move away so she won't be tempted to go back to Manon. Marg and Sue get along, and it will be good for Marg to have some company."

"Perhaps they'll fall in love," mused Raven, giving Harry a hug.

Harry didn't think so, at least not for a long, long time. Sue had a lot of healing to do before something like that could happen. "Maybe."

"I saw Judy sitting with her girlfriend on the other side of the room," Raven said.

Harry's behind was beginning to go numb. She pulled her legs up and tugged Raven closer to her. "So did I. But they ignored me. Judy didn't even look in my direction when she and Sarah left."

"Good riddance," Raven muttered.

Harry smiled. "You're pretty tough on people."

"And you always give people the benefit of the doubt."

"It's a small thing to give them, after all," Harry murmured.

There was a long silence, and then Raven asked, "So, what are you going to give me?"

"What do you mean?" Harry asked, but she already knew. The time had come. She opened her mouth and then closed it again.

Raven stopped rocking. "Say something. Anything."

"I love you."

"And I love you."

"So how would you feel about living in a guesthouse in the southern-most city in the United States?" Harry asked.

Raven's fervent kiss was the only answer Harry needed.

More entertaining, fast-paced mysteries in the acclaimed Harriet Hubbley Mystery Series by Jackie Manthorne

Final Take: A Harriet Hubbley Mystery

"Demonstrates that Manthorne is a natural, a born storyteller with a flair for creating memorable characters and "page-turner" mystery fiction." *The Midwest Book Review*

Nominated for a 1997 Lambda Literary Award in the lesbian mystery category.

ISBN 0-921881-41-X $10.95

Last Resort: A Harriet Hubbley Mystery

"*Last Resort* is a novel with all the twists and hidden corners one would expect." *Lesbian Review of Books*

"… delivers character, plot and setting." *Capital XTRA!*

ISBN 0-921881-34-7 $10.95

Deadly Reunion: A Harriet Hubbley Mystery

"Manthorne has a clean, crisp style and a heroine likeable enough to create something of a following." *Bay Windows*, U.S.A.

ISBN 0-921881-32-0 $10.95

Jackie Manthorne is the author of two collections of short stories, *Fascination and Other Bar Stories* and *Without Wings*, as well as the Harriet Hubbley Mystery Series (all from gynergy books). Her writing has appeared in numerous magazines and anthologies, including *Lesbian Bedtime Stories II* (Tough Dove Books) and *By Word of Mouth: Lesbians Write the Erotic* (gynergy books). She is also the editor of *Canadian Women and AIDS: Beyond the Statistics* (Les Éditions Communiqu'Elles). She lives in Toronto, where she writes full time.

Best of gynergy books

Bordering, *Luanne Armstrong*. Louise is "bordering": on coming out as a lesbian, on imagining her future, on leaving the small town that keeps her pinned down. But before she can cross over to a new life, she must face up to the old. ISBN 0-921881-35-5 $10.95

By Word of Mouth: Lesbians Write the Erotic, *Lee Fleming (ed.).* "Contains plenty of sexy good writing and furthers the desperately needed honest discussion of what we mean by 'erotic' and by 'lesbian.'" *Sinister Wisdom* ISBN 0-921881-06-1 $10.95/$12.95 U.S.

Hot Licks: Lesbian Musicians of Note, *Lee Fleming (ed.).* From the beginning of women's music in the '60s to the centre stage of mainstream concert halls in the '90s, lesbian musicians are coming out. In *Hot Licks*, they proudly and eloquently reveal their passions and politics. Beautiful design, large format and high quality photographs make this the ideal giftbook. "A handsome assemblage of biographies, discographies and song lyrics from famous and up-and-coming lesbian performers." *The Advocate* ISBN 0-921881-42-8 $24.95

Lesbian Parenting: Living with Pride & Prejudice, *Katherine Arnup (ed.).* Here is the perfect primer for lesbian parents, and a helpful resource for their families and friends. "Thoughtful, provocative and passionate. A brave and necessary book." *Sandra Butler* ISBN 0-921881-33-9 $19.95

To Sappho, My Sister: Lesbian Sisters Write About Their Lives, *Lee Fleming (ed.).* This one-of-a-kind anthology includes the stories of both well-known and less famous siblings from three continents, in a compelling portrait of lesbian sisterhood. "This book will hold you captive." *Curve* ISBN 0-921881-36-3 $16.95

gynergy books titles are available at quality bookstores. Ask for our titles at your favourite local bookstore. Individual, prepaid orders may be sent to: **gynergy books**, P.O. Box 2023, Charlottetown, Prince Edward Island, Canada, C1A 7N7. Please add postage and handling ($3.00 for the first book and $1.00 for each additional book) to your order. Canadian residents add 7% GST to the total amount. GST registration number R104383120. Prices are subject to change without notice.